NOWHERE TO RUN

Emily was lost in the sound of the new cymbals when her stepmother opened the door to the studio. "Emily!" Karen yelled angrily. "I have *finally* gotten the baby to fall asleep, and now you've woken her up again!"

Emily stared at her stepmother. "But we agreed that between four o'clock and—"

"I don't care *what* we agreed," Karen said acidly. "I have absolutely had it with this constant noise, young lady. If you refuse to cooperate with a few simple rules—"

"But I'm *not* refusing!" Emily cried. "You just keep changing the rules on me all the time! Karen, I can't just—"

"Oh, do what you please," Karen said, heading for the stairs. "Just make sure you cut out the noise. Because the next time you bother little Karrie—I mean it, Emily, the *next* time . . ."

Bantam Books in the Sweet Valley High Series
Ask your bookseller for the books you have missed

SWEET VALLEY HIGH

NOWHERE TO RUN

Written by
Kate William

Created by
FRANCINE PASCAL

BANTAM BOOKS
TORONTO · NEW YORK · LONDON · SYDNEY · AUCKLAND

RL 6, IL age 12 and up

NOWHERE TO RUN
A Bantam Book / January 1986

Sweet Valley High is a trademark of Francine Pascal

Conceived by Francine Pascal

Produced by Cloverdale Press, Inc.,
133 Fifth Avenue, New York, N.Y. 10003

Cover art by James Mathewuse

ISBN 0-553-25299-2

Published simultaneously in the United States and Canada

PRINTED IN THE UNITED STATES OF AMERICA

O   0 9 8 7 6 5 4 3 2 1

NOWHERE TO RUN

One

"I'm so excited!" Jessica Wakefield exclaimed, her aquamarine eyes shining as she faced her twin across the cafeteria table. The twins had found a relatively quiet corner of the crowded lunchroom in Sweet Valley High so they could make plans for the biggest family event in ages—a three-week visit from their grandparents. "Do you realize, Liz, that tonight's the night? Grandma and Grandpa Wakefield are finally going to be here!"

Elizabeth laughed and picked up her tuna sandwich. "From the sound of it, Jess, the hours between now and then are really going to drag for you."

"Can I help it?" Jessica demanded. "Liz, we haven't seen them in *ages*. I'd be completely inhuman not to be counting the minutes till they're here!"

Elizabeth was looking forward to her grand-

1

parents' visit just as much as Jessica was, but as usual her twin was functioning by what their parents laughingly called Jessica Standard Time. Jessica never wore a watch, and it was next to impossible to convince her that minutes mattered when it came to getting to an appointment on time—or do anything Jessica considered dull. But when Jessica was looking forward to something, it was almost impossible for her just to sit still and wait. Elizabeth loved teasing her twin for being so impatient, but secretly she considered her sister's enthusiasm one of her best characteristics.

Looking at her sister's face across the cafeteria table was like staring into a mirror. Elizabeth and Jessica were identical in almost every detail, from their sparkling, blue-green eyes and shoulder-length, sun-streaked golden hair to the tiny dimple in the left cheek each showed when she smiled. They were both five feet six inches tall with model-slim, size-six figures. "One of the wonderful things about having a twin," Jessica was fond of remarking as she investigated her sister's closet, "is that identical sizes means twice as many clothes!"

Actually, there wasn't much in Elizabeth's closet that interested Jessica. Elizabeth struck her as being too conservative, and the truth was that Jessica loved change and excitement. And not just in her wardrobe, either. Whatever she was doing, whether it was learning a new cheer with the cheerleading squad or flirting with a new boy, Jessica threw herself into it. The only problem was that she sometimes got carried away, and got into trouble. In fact, sometimes Elizabeth thought "Trouble" was her twin's middle name.

But as troublesome as Jessica sometimes was, Elizabeth could never stay angry with her for more than a few minutes. There were times when Elizabeth couldn't for the life of her figure out what her twin was really thinking, but she knew that the bottom line was that she'd always stick by her twin, no matter what. And she knew Jessica would always stick by her, too.

"Liz, I have the most wonderful idea!" Jessica said, pushing her carton of yogurt away and starting to peel a wrapper off an ice-cream sandwich. "Why don't we both go straight home after school and decorate the house for Grandma and Grandpa?"

"That's a great idea," Elizabeth said, picturing the living room festooned with streamers. But the next minute her face fell. "I can't, though," she added, noticing out of the corner of her eye that two fellow juniors, Emily Mayer and Dana Larson, were setting their trays down at the next table. "I promised Mr. Collins I'd do some work at *The Oracle* this afternoon. I have a feeling I won't be able to get home till about five-thirty."

Mr. Collins was the faculty adviser to the student newspaper, for which Elizabeth was a reporter and columnist.

Jessica looked disappointed. "How you can stand working in that office is beyond me," she grumbled. "That place is a mess!"

"Jessica," Elizabeth said reproachfully, "do you think Barbara Walters ever got this from *her* sister?"

"Never mind," Jessica said, her expression clearing. "I'll take care of all the decorating myself, Liz."

"You'd better go easy on the living room," Elizabeth told her. "Mom spent all weekend cleaning it, remember?"

Jessica's eyebrows shot up. "Are you trying to suggest I don't know how to decorate a room?" she demanded, hurt. "I just think Grandma and Grandpa need some kind of special welcome," she added.

Elizabeth laughed. "I'm sure you'll do a wonderful job."

She couldn't believe it had been over a year since she and Jessica had last seen their grandparents. Sweet Valley, California, was a long way from the town in Michigan where they lived, but even so!

"Grandma said she's going to take us shopping," Jessica was saying dreamily. "Remember? She said she wants to buy us a complete outfit each. And Grandpa says he's going to take us out for a special dinner—just the two of us and Grandma and Grandpa!"

"It'll be so good to see them," Elizabeth said distractedly, taking a sip of her root beer.

"You're not even listening to me," Jessica said, pouting.

Elizabeth frowned and didn't answer. Jessica was right. Her mind was only partly on the conversation they were having. But it wasn't because she didn't care about the arrangements their grandparents had made. It was just that the conversation at the next table was getting louder and more intense, and Elizabeth couldn't help overhearing snatches of it. She didn't know Emily Mayer that well, but from the look on the girl's face, it was obvious that she was upset.

Emily was petite, about five feet two inches tall, and slender, with long, dark, wavy hair. Her hazel eyes were flecked with green and gray lights that sparkled when she was feeling emotional—or when she was deeply involved in her music.

Emily was the drummer for The Droids, the Sweet Valley High rock group, and Dana, the head singer for the group, had once told Elizabeth that the group would be lost without her. The group took their music very seriously—and for good reason. They had gotten quite a bit of attention in the community and had even played at a few local clubs.

"I still think it would be fun," Dana was

saying, shaking her head at Emily. "Babies are so cute! And little Karrie is cuter than most."

"You wouldn't think she was so cute if you had to live with her," Emily said coldly. "All she does is scream and make a complete mess. Besides—"

"You're not being fair," Dana interrupted. "Karrie's so sweet! I'd give anything to have a baby sister. I think you're lucky."

"Stepsister," Emily said pointedly. "She's my stepsister, Dana, not my sister. And believe me, there's a big difference!"

Elizabeth toyed thoughtfully with the wrapper from her straw. Emily really sounded worked up, she thought. Elizabeth had noticed that Emily seemed tense recently. She was jumpy, as if something were bugging her all the time. *Oh, well*, Elizabeth thought. *It's none of my business, and I shouldn't be eavesdropping!*

Just then Dana Larson leaned across the table. "Liz, wouldn't *you* love having a little baby around to play with all the time? Help me convince Emily she's got the wrong attitude!"

Emily looked embarrassed. Elizabeth could tell the last thing she wanted was to turn a private conversation into a group discussion. "I don't know," Elizabeth said lightly, trying not to interfere. "A new baby around the house is probably quite an adjustment." She smiled at Emily, and the girl smiled back at her gratefully.

"It is," she said quickly, staring down at her

6

hands. "At first I thought I *did* have an attitude problem," she admitted, "but now I realize that it isn't me that has a problem. It's my stepmother, Karen."

Silence followed this announcement. Elizabeth had no idea what to say.

"But Karen's such a sweetheart!" Dana interjected, staring at Emily. "She's always going out of her way to be so nice to everyone!"

"Everyone but me," Emily corrected her. "Look, I know what you're thinking," she added quickly. "I probably sound completely paranoid, right? But that isn't how it is." She took a deep breath, obviously fighting for control. "The truth is, Karen really has it in for me. She always did, but it wasn't so bad before Karrie was born. Now it's obvious that she wants to get rid of me." Emily blinked, her hazel eyes filling with tears. "She wants me out of the house so she can have my father all to herself."

Dana gasped. "Emily! Are you sure? You're sure you're not just—"

"I've never been more sure of anything in my whole life," Emily said quietly. She stood up, gripping the edge of the table so hard that her knuckles turned white. "What I'm sure of," she added grimly, "is what to do about it. Sweet Valley is my home—and I'm not going to let her kick me out!"

"Emily, wait!" Dana exclaimed, jumping up

to run after the distraught girl as she hurried out of the crowded cafeteria.

"Wow," Jessica said, her eyes widening. "What was *that* all about?"

"I don't know," Elizabeth said grimly. "But it doesn't sound like things are exactly rosy over at the Mayers' house these days!"

It was four o'clock, and Elizabeth was proofreading her column for that week's *Oracle* when the door to the newspaper office swung open. "Liz!" Mr. Collins exclaimed, setting down the box he was carrying. "I'm sorry I'm late, but I had to help out a few students after class."

Elizabeth smiled warmly at Mr. Collins. Aside from devoting so much of his free time to being faculty adviser for the school paper, he was one of the most all-around generous teachers in the school. It was no wonder he was so popular among his students. "I'm glad you're here," Elizabeth told him. "I could use some help on the article I'm writing on the tenure system. Any ideas?"

"Lots," Mr. Collins told her, smiling. "But first, I'm afraid I have to ask for your help. I know you're busy, but Emily Mayer asked me if anyone on the paper could help her try out for the editorial staff, and I told her I'd ask you."

"Emily!" Elizabeth exclaimed. "But why does she want to work for *The Oracle*? She's a musician, not a journalist!"

Mr. Collins shrugged. "I didn't ask, but she seemed very eager. And I know how patient you are, Liz. You'd probably be able to help her out a great deal."

"I'd be glad to," Elizabeth said.

"Great! As a matter of fact, she's supposed to come by any minute. Do you think you could spend a little time showing her around?"

Elizabeth laughed. "No time like the present," she told him, setting her note pad down.

Mr. Collins glanced down at his watch and frowned. "Would you mind if I left you alone with Emily for about fifteen minutes? I've got to run over and straighten out a scheduling problem in the office."

"Sure," Elizabeth told him. "Is there anything in particular I should tell her?"

"Just give her a general tour," Mr. Collins suggested. "Oh," he added a second later, looking searchingly at Elizabeth. "You might want to give her a little moral support, too. I get the impression she could use it."

Elizabeth was about to ask Mr. Collins what he meant, but before she could say a word, the door swung open again, and Emily hurried into the room. Elizabeth caught her breath when she saw the girl. She looked awful. She was pale, and her eyes were red-rimmed. It was obvious she'd been crying.

Mr. Collins gave Emily a long look before leaving the office. "Can you stick around when

Liz is done with her tour?" he asked. "I'd like to talk to you."

Emily nodded and took a seat. "He's so nice," she said softly when he had left the room, closing the door behind him. "He reminds me of. . ."

"Of what?" Elizabeth asked gently. She didn't want to probe, but it struck her that Emily wanted to confide in someone.

Emily shrugged. "He reminds me a little bit of the way my father used to be. Before he married Karen," she added.

"Emily," Elizabeth said, "you don't have to answer this if you don't want to, but I was wondering why you were interested in joining the paper. Is writing something you've cared about for a long time?"

Emily bit her lip. "As a matter of fact, I don't know much about writing," she admitted. "I've never been all that good at expressing myself on paper. It's much easier for me to do that when I'm playing my drums."

"I thought so," Elizabeth said. "Why *The Oracle*, then?" She wondered if things were so bad at home that Emily was just trying to find things to keep her busy, though the school newspaper still didn't seem to be the most likely option.

"To tell you the truth, this is really my stepmother's idea." Emily sighed. "Liz, can I talk to you? I don't want to burden anyone, but I feel like I'm going to explode if I don't confide in someone! And I've always admired you so much," she added wistfully. "You seem so to-gether all the time—like you never have any problems."

"I *always* have problems," Elizabeth told her, smiling. "But all the same, you can talk to me about whatever you want, Emily. I may not have any advice for you, but I'll certainly listen."

"Thanks," Emily said gratefully. "The thing is that Karen, my stepmother, has been trying to convince my father that I need to go to board-ing school." She shuddered, her eyes darken-ing as she thought about it. "She says I need the discipline. I don't know exactly what she means by that, but I know what she wants. She wants to get me out of the house. At first I was so angry I couldn't stand it. But now I'm really afraid of Karen. My father's so madly in love with her that he doesn't realize what she's trying to do."

"Emily, that's awful!" Elizabeth cried.

Emily sighed. "I've been living with this for a while," she said quietly. "It isn't getting any better, either. And I've faced the fact now that I have to start making some changes in my life or I *won't* have any choice. She really will get me sent away. And I just couldn't stand that."

"What does *The Oracle* have to do with that?" Elizabeth asked gently.

"Karen can't stand my music," she explained. "She thinks it's all just noise. And she really hates the drums. She doesn't like it when I practice at home, because of the baby. And I can understand that. But she's taken it even further. She's convinced my father that The Droids are all really wild—that they're a bad influence."

"That's ridiculous!" Elizabeth burst out.

Emily sighed. "Liz, right now I don't want to think about what's right or wrong. I just want to do what she wants me to do so she doesn't send me away."

"And she wants you to join the newspaper?"

Emily nodded. "She's always telling me how much more intellectual writing is than music. So that's why I'm here," she added, smiling so simply that Elizabeth thought her heart would break for the girl. "I don't have much left in the world, Liz. I lost my mother years ago. All I have is my father—and Sweet Valley. And now Karen's threatening to take both things away. My feeling is that it's worth anything to keep her from doing that. So I'm going to try things her way for a while." Emily drew a long, shuddering breath. "I figure," she added quietly, "that it's my only chance. But if this doesn't work, Liz, I don't know what I'll do!"

Two

As Emily walked home after her meeting with Mr. Collins, she barely noticed the warmth of the sun on her bare arms or the sweet smell of the flowers blooming on the bushes lining the street. Ordinarily Emily was sensitive to the beauty of the neighborhood. It was one of the things about Sweet Valley that meant so much to her. The things she liked best about the town were things few other people noticed. Like the way the wind sounded by the ocean at night, she thought, smiling sadly. Or the little rainbows the sun made through the sprinklers.

Emily wished the lump in her throat would go away. But she couldn't get over the sadness that had been growing stronger and stronger since Karen had brought little Karrie home from the hospital. Before that, things had been bad, but bearable. Sure, she knew Karen didn't exactly love her. But she had told herself over and over again that this was the woman her father had chosen. And she wanted her father to be happy. Especially after what had happened with her mother.

Emily still couldn't think about her mother without getting tears in her eyes. Nobody at school knew about it. Emily had told everyone that her mother had died when she was very young. They didn't know the truth—that Mrs. Mayer had just taken off one day, leaving Emily and her father alone.

What kind of mother just took off and left her husband and her little girl? As far as Emily was concerned, her mother might as well be dead.

Still, in many ways the years following her mother's departure had been happy ones for Emily. Ronald Mayer had been wonderful to his only child, sharing almost all of her interests, taking her with him when he traveled, trying his hardest to be both mother and father to her. In fact, it was her father who first introduced her to the drums. He had played them when he was a boy. Only he wasn't as serious about music as Emily became.

Her father had been thrilled by Emily's interest in music. And it wasn't just interest, either. She had real talent. That was what Cliff Green, her drum teacher, said. When she'd joined The Droids, her father had been so excited! He went to every gig they had, even some of the school dances, just to hear her play.

From time to time Emily had wondered if her father would ever remarry. He had divorced her mother soon after she had left, and Emily knew he must be lonely, that he must wish he had someone with whom to share his life. But when he started dating Karen she couldn't believe anything would ever come of it. Karen was . . . well, she wasn't the sort of woman Emily would have picked out for her father. She was nice enough. And pretty, too, though her looks were too fussy for Emily's taste.

But Karen was the only child of a wealthy couple, and she was used to getting a lot of attention. Almost from the beginning she'd made it clear that she thought Emily was spoiled rotten, and she wanted to put an end to that. *She* wanted the attention, and she didn't want Emily sharing the spotlight with her.

Emily felt uneasy about Karen. She sensed that the woman didn't care for her, but all the same Karen always put on a great act when other people, especially Emily's father, were around.

Still, when her father told her he and Karen were getting married, Emily had convinced herself everything would be all right. Now that Karen knew she was going to be Mrs. Mayer, maybe she'd feel more secure about things. Maybe she'd ease up on Emily.

Emily sighed. *But I was wrong. I was kidding myself.*

Oh, in the very beginning things were a little better. Karen was so thrilled when she first moved into the house that nothing seemed to dampen her spirits. But it didn't take very long before she started picking little fights with Emily. It seemed as though nothing Emily did was right. If she went out, Karen objected to her friends or claimed she was staying out too late. If she stayed in, Karen wondered why she didn't have an active social life. It was ridiculous!

Well, that was two years ago. And during the past two years Emily had grown accustomed to her stepmother's erratic behavior. She had done her best not to lose heart, even when Karen came between her and her father, telling him things that were . . . well, if not exactly untrue, certainly biased.

Then Karen got pregnant—and anyone would have thought that Karen was the only woman who had ever become pregnant. She quit her job immediately and lay around the house, demanding attention, complaining like crazy, and ordering Emily around all the time. It reached the point where Emily dreaded going home after school. Karen had always been hard to deal with, but after she became pregnant, she was impossible.

Even Emily's father noticed the change in his wife, and he spoke to his daughter about it on several occasions. But Mr. Mayer loved Karen so much that he was blind to weaknesses in her character. "Just bear with her," he told Emily, smiling. "It's hard work having a baby!"

Emily had tried her hardest. And she'd waited, figuring things had to get better.

But they hadn't. Karen had grown more and more preoccupied with her unborn baby, spending almost every waking minute sewing little booties for it or reading books on child care. Even worse, she had turned into a fanatic about cleanliness. The Mayers' house had always looked comfortable and lived-in, but Karen suddenly decided that it was unsanitary. She had convinced Emily's father to hire a housekeeper, and within weeks there wasn't a speck of dust anywhere. "It looks like a museum in here," Emily had grumbled.

"We have to keep things clean," Karen had replied cheerfully. "Things are going to be different around here, Emily, now that the baby's on its way!"

Well, I can't say she didn't warn me! Emily said to herself, shifting her book bag from one shoulder to the other. *Karen spent months telling me how different everything was going to be. And she's right. Things sure are different!*

It seemed to Emily that the entire world revolved around Karrie. When Karrie cried, everyone had to run to see what was wrong. If Karrie was tired, everyone had to be quiet so she could sleep. And if Karrie was awake, which was much more likely, it was considered some kind of cardinal sin not to pay attention to her every single second.

Actually Emily was as fascinated by Karrie as everyone else was. How could she help it? Karrie *was* sweet. She was almost eight months old now and she had enormous blue eyes. She was soft and cuddly, and so vulnerable. All Emily had to do was pick her up and bury her face in Karrie's sweet-smelling, talcum-dusted neck to feel as if everything were worthwhile.

No, Karrie wasn't the problem. Emily had realized it was going to be a big adjustment having a baby around the house, but the compromises weren't actually that demanding.

It was Karen who was making her life miserable. No sooner had she brought little Karrie home from the hospital than Karen had suddenly begun hinting that Emily might be better off at a boarding school. At first Emily had thought she was just talking, that she'd forget all about it. But it soon became obvious that Karen meant business. She had convinced Mr. Mayer that Emily needed stricter curfews, that she was hanging out with kids who were a bad influence on her. She'd gotten him worried about Emily. Then she had suggested that the solution was to send Emily to boarding school!

Emily didn't know much about boarding schools. But she did know this: Sweet Valley was her home, and nothing in the world was going to make her leave.

"Nothing," she said out loud, her brow wrinkling with determination. Not even Karen.

Leaving Sweet Valley was simply out of the question. Especially since Dan Scott had come into the picture. It wasn't that anything had exactly *happened* between Emily and Dan. They were just friends—really good friends. He was the bass guitar player for The Droids, and lately he and Emily had been practicing together a lot and talking about all sorts of things, such as music, and the future. They were growing close.

Emily wasn't sure exactly what she felt for Dan. All she knew was that she'd like the chance to know him better. *Just one more reason to make it clear to Dad that boarding school is the last thing I need*, Emily thought.

Emily knew how tough it was going to be to persuade her father that Karen was wrong. But she also knew she had no other choice. And the time for convincing him, she told herself, was long overdue. It was time to show Karen that Emily Mayer wasn't about to run out of town!

"Dinner's ready!" Alice Wakefield called, stepping into the living room with a smile on her pretty face. Blond-haired and blue-eyed, Mrs. Wakefield was slim and young looking. She could easily have passed for the twins' older sister. Mrs. Wakefield was an interior designer,

19

and her work was both rewarding and demanding.

"I don't know how you do it, Alice," Grandpa Wakefield said appreciatively, his dark eyes twinkling as he surveyed the food spread out on the dining-room table. "How you manage to work full time and still prepare a dinner like this is beyond me!"

"The world has changed, Bob," Grandma Wakefield teased him as the family sat down at the table. "This *does* put me to shame, though, Alice," she admitted. "I'm afraid poor Bob hasn't had a good home-cooked meal in ages. We've been relying on fast food and take-out Chinese ever since I went back to school."

"I think it's wonderful that you decided to go back," Elizabeth said enthusiastically. "Tell me what you're doing your research on, Grandma."

"Your grandmother," Grandma Wakefield told her, "is the oldest student in the Ph.D. program in American history at the University of Michigan! Sometimes I wonder what I'm doing," she said, chuckling. "All these college kids come in with their knapsacks and those little tape players they listen to—you know, with those little headphones—"

"Walkmen," Jessica filled in for her.

"And there I am! But you know, I really love studying. I always have," she confided, her blue eyes twinkling as she smoothed back her short-cropped, silvery hair. "I'm learning so many fascinating things about this country's history, too. If you girls could put up with it, I'd love to take you for a drive up the coast. There's a museum about an hour north of here that has a wonderful exhibit I'd love to see."

"That sounds great, Grandma," Elizabeth said. To her surprise, Jessica's face lit up the minute their grandmother suggested the outing. History wasn't exactly Jessica's favorite subject. But it was clear that their grandparents could suggest going to the moon and Jessica would still be delighted.

In fact, Elizabeth hadn't seen her twin behaving this way for about as long as she could remember. Jessica looked absolutely enchanted.

"You're spoiling us, you know," Grandpa Wakefield teased her. "First you put up all those beautiful decorations. And now you flatter us with all this attention! Better take it easy, Jess. You may never be able to get rid of us!"

"That would be wonderful," Jessica said solemnly, reaching for the salad bowl. "I mean it!" she added indignantly when her father burst out laughing. "Everyone I know has grandparents who live nearby. I bet I'm the only kid at school who gets to see her grandparents only once a year."

"No, you're not," Elizabeth corrected her. "What about me?"

"OK, you two," Mr. Wakefield said, leaning back in his chair, his dark eyes twinkling. "Quit trying to make your grandparents feel guilty. They're just trying," he told his parents, "to make sure you don't change your mind about that trip to Hampshire Place you promised them."

Hampshire Place was a brand-new mall in a neighboring town, and the twins had been looking forward to seeing it for weeks. But they'd been saving it so they could see it for the first time with their grandparents.

"Oh, we haven't forgotten about that, have we, Bob?" Grandma Wakefield said, buttering a second piece of bread. "How does Thursday afternoon sound?"

"Thursday's great!" the twins said in unison.

"Grandma, can we go on that drive up the coast this weekend?" Jessica asked, her eyes shining. "I can't believe I'm going to have a real live professor for a grandmother! Will you help me with my history paper for Mr. Jaworski?"

"Jessica," Elizabeth said reproachfully, "Grandma's on vacation. She doesn't want to work on a history paper!"

"Nonsense," Grandma Wakefield declared, settling back in her chair and smiling. "I told you, girls. History is my favorite thing in the world—after my grandchildren, that is. I'd be delighted to help, and we can go anywhere you want this weekend."

"Well," Mrs. Wakefield said briskly, getting up from the table. "It sounds like you're all going to have a busy week! Can I bring anyone dessert or coffee?"

Her mother sounded tired, Elizabeth thought, glancing at Alice Wakefield out of the corner of her eye. She looked kind of tired, too.

But Elizabeth's reflection was interrupted by the sound of her grandfather's voice as he began recounting the adventures he and Grandma Wakefield had had at the airport. He was such a good storyteller, and his descriptions of people were so lively and amusing that he had them all breaking up with laughter.

Jessica's right, Elizabeth thought to herself. It was wonderful having her grandparents there. It made everything seem special, as if it were a holiday. If only they really *could* live in Sweet Valley all the time!

But in a way, grandparents who lived far away were even more special. Elizabeth knew Jessica felt the same way deep down. This way they could look forward to the magic weeks when their grandparents came to visit.

Catching Jessica's eye, Elizabeth was convinced her twin felt just as she did: They would both do everything they could to prolong the magic and enjoy their grandparents' visit to the hilt!

Three

"Emily," Mr. Mayer said, standing in the doorway to her bedroom and loosening his tie as he spoke. "I was wondering if the two of us could have a talk before dinner. Are you busy right now?"

It was Tuesday evening, and Emily had been leafing through the notes Elizabeth had given her on *The Oracle*, trying to come up with an idea for a trial article. "No, not really," she told her father, trying to keep the frustration out of her voice. *I don't want to try out for* The Oracle, she had been thinking unhappily. *I'm not good at this sort of thing! I should be practicing that new routine Dan and I worked out instead.*

"Listen," her father said, rocking back and forth slightly on the balls of his feet, the way he always did when he was nervous or upset about something. "Karen told me that the two of you have been having a disagreement about your curfew. She asked me to talk to you about it."

Emily bit her lip. *Here we go,* she thought, setting down the sheaf of papers and swiveling in her chair to face her father. It looked as if Karen had cornered her father the minute he'd gotten home from the office. And as much as Emily had dreaded the confrontation she had a feeling might be coming, she was glad they'd be able to clear the air at last.

"You always said you didn't believe in curfews," Emily reminded him. "Remember? As long as I used my judgment and didn't start acting irresponsibly."

Mr. Mayer sighed and ran his hands through his graying hair. "You're right, Em," he admitted. "That's exactly what I said. And I know it must seem pretty confusing to you that this is all coming up now, after we had our own system worked out. But you have Karen's feelings to consider now, too, honey. And she feels— well, she feels it would be better for you if you had a fixed schedule to go by."

Emily took a deep breath. "What sort of schedule?"

"We've both given this a lot of thought," her father told her. "And we decided that it wouldn't be unreasonable to expect you home by ten o'clock on weeknights and midnight on weekends. Does that seem fair to you?"

"Fair!" Emily stared at her father, the color

draining from her face. For a minute she was almost too flustered to speak. "But, Dad, The Droids practice until ten-thirty or eleven on Mondays and Wednesdays. It takes so long to set up all the equipment after dinner, and it's a complete waste if we don't get in at least two hours' practice!"

"Emily," her father said quietly, "you have a baby sister to think about now, too. You may not realize it, but when you come home late, you wake her up. That isn't fair, is it?"

Emily felt her eyes stinging with tears. "But, Dad, what am I supposed to do about The Droids? You know how much it means to me to play with them!"

She knew she was hitting a nerve when she said that. Her father had always been proud of her musical ability. *It's so strange,* Emily thought. *How can he go back on everything he ever taught me?* The idea of a fixed curfew seemed foreign to Emily. After all, she had had to assume certain kinds of responsibility at a very young age. She had helped her father run the household for years. In exchange, her father treated her with respect. He knew she would never keep unreasonably late hours. He trusted her judgment. But Karen didn't. And lately, whatever Karen felt was law.

"Dad," Emily tried again, "don't you think this is just a little bit unfair? I appreciate how

Karen feels," she added quickly, "but don't you think—"

"Emily," her father said abruptly, his expression darkening, "I want you to stop giving Karen a hard time. She's got her hands full as it is. She needs you to help her, not to make things worse. Now I don't want to hear another word about this curfew matter. As far as I'm concerned, the case is closed."

Emily stared at him. She couldn't believe this was her father talking. He sounded so cold, so remote.

For the first time, Emily actually felt afraid. She realized now that she couldn't reach her father anymore. He didn't believe anything she said. It was Karen's word against hers, and it was obvious who was winning out.

And if that was how it was, Emily thought miserably, what was to keep her father from believing Karen when she told him that Sweet Valley High was the wrong kind of school for Emily, that she really needed to go to a boarding school?

Emily had never felt so helpless in her life. And she had no one to turn to, either. She couldn't dump all her family problems on Dan. He'd never be interested in her if he found out what a messed-up home life she had!

But she knew she couldn't handle the situation alone; she needed help. And she just had no idea where, if anywhere, that help was going to come from.

"Emily, the phone's for you!" Karen called from down the hall. It was almost ten o'clock. *Who could be calling this late?* Emily wondered, picking up the extension in her bedroom.

"Emily?" a nervous voice began. "This is Dan. I was wondering why you didn't come to practice tonight. We were supposed to meet at Max's house, remember?"

Emily clapped her hand to her forehead. She had forgotten The Droids had arranged a special rehearsal for that night. In all the recent confusion, it had just slipped her mind.

"I forgot," she confided. "Dan, was everyone furious that I wasn't there?"

"I covered for you," Dan said shyly. "I told them you were coming down with a cold, and that probably had something to do with your not showing up. Anyway, we didn't get very much practicing done. Mostly we just worked on that new song we were doing last night. Hey," he said, as if something had just occurred to him, "maybe we could get together sometime, just the two of us, and I could go over it with you."

"That'd be great, Dan," Emily said happily. "I'd really like that."

"How about this weekend? Maybe we could get together Friday night."

"Friday night would be just fine," Emily told him, trying to keep the elation out of her voice. For several minutes after she'd replaced the receiver on the hook, Emily sat perfectly still, thinking about Dan Scott.

Dan was almost seventeen, with sun-streaked, baby-fine, brown hair and gray eyes that crinkled up at the corners when he smiled. He wasn't conventionally handsome, but Emily had always liked his looks. He had a wonderful smile, too, she thought. Very shy and sweet.

Friday night, Emily mused. *I wonder what will happen. Does Dan really like me, or is he just—*

"Emily, are you off the phone?" Karen called, interrupting her reverie.

Emily was determined not to let her stepmother spoil the good mood Dan's phone call had produced. "Come on in," she said cheerfully, opening her bedroom door.

Unfortunately, Karen's expression as she came into the room suggested that *her* mood was not too good. "Who was that on the phone?" she demanded. "Didn't I tell you that Karrie wakes up every time it rings?"

"It was a friend from school," Emily mumbled, staring at her carpet. "He doesn't know about Karrie."

"Well, make sure you tell him if he's going to be calling again," Karen snapped. "I'm so tired," she complained, leaning against the door and closing her eyes dramatically. "I had no idea a baby was such hard work!"

Emily tried to look sympathetic, but she could feel herself stiffening the way she always did when Karen went into one of her routines. Maybe she shouldn't blame Karen for it. Karen's overprotective parents had always done everything for her. She had been taken care of so well that it seemed that everything she had to do herself was a chore for her now.

For one thing, Karen didn't seem to know anything about running a house. She couldn't balance the checkbooks or do the grocery shopping without botching it all up. She was a terrible cook, and she had no idea how to perform even the simplest tasks, such as cleaning the oven or even emptying a vacuum-cleaner bag.

And instead of being grateful when Emily showed her how to do certain things, she got resentful about it. Emily had just about given up. But Karen had Karrie now. She didn't care about things like cooking or shopping now that the baby was here.

"Your father has a wonderful idea," Karen said when it became clear that Emily wasn't going to ask her exactly what made little Karrie so utterly exhausting. "He picked up some theater tickets for this weekend. He thinks I need to get out of the house, and I think he's right. Anyway, I told him you'd stay with Karrie. I

31

just don't trust anybody else with her—and you're so capable, Em."

Emily felt a little warning signal go off inside. Whenever her stepmother complimented her or called her by her nickname, she knew trouble was coming.

"What night this weekend?" she asked, trying to keep her voice calm.

"Friday," Karen said, looking surprised. "Why? You don't have plans, do you?"

Emily bit her lip. "As a matter of fact, I do."

"Can you change them? Your dad already bought the tickets, Em, and they cost a lot of money."

Emily knew from experience what the pout on her stepmother's face meant: *You'd better agree with me fast, or there's going to be trouble.*

"I've made plans with a friend," Emily said slowly. "I might be able to change them, but I'd really rather—"

"Great!" Karen exclaimed, cutting her off. "Thank you so much, Em. I don't know what we'd do without you!"

Fighting for control, Emily stared at her step-mother. She felt trapped. Either she had to make a big scene, drag her father into it, and insist she wouldn't change her plans—which would make Karen even more serious about trying to get her out of the house—or she had to just give in, which would be like letting Karen know that she could walk all over her.

It seemed that Karen had Emily exactly where she wanted her. And Emily couldn't see any way out.

"Not the jack, Jessica," her grandfather said reprovingly. "Remember, face cards are worth ten points each. Why don't you throw out your five instead?"

The twins were sitting on the floor in the living room, engaged in a furious practice session for a card game their grandmother had invented.

"It's sort of a variation on poker," their grandmother told them, taking her glasses out of her pocket and putting them on so she could study her cards. "Lucky in cards, unlucky in love." She sighed and put her hand down. "Well, I guess it's worth it," she joked, smiling at Grandpa Wakefield. "I'd rather have your grandfather than four aces any day!"

"Looks like things are going pretty smoothly in there," Ned Wakefield said, joining his wife out on the patio surrounding the swimming pool in the backyard. It was a fragrant, balmy evening, and Mrs. Wakefield was relaxing on a deck chair, an unopened novel on her lap.

"You can say that again!" Mrs. Wakefield said. "I haven't gotten a minute alone with Jessica or Elizabeth since your parents arrived. It's as if they have a monopoly on their affection," she added.

"Hey," Mr. Wakefield said reprovingly. "You're not really feeling sensitive about the twins, are you?"

Mrs. Wakefield was quiet for a minute. "No." She sighed. "It's just—well, they seem so happy now that your parents are here. I guess it's just been making me do a little bit of thinking, that's all."

"What sort of thinking?" Mr. Wakefield pressed her.

"Ned," Mrs. Wakefield said seriously, leaning forward on her chair to look directly at him, "do you think I've been neglecting the girls lately?"

"Neglecting them?" Mr. Wakefield burst out laughing. "Alice, are you kidding? You're a wonderful mother," he assured her.

Mrs. Wakefield looked thoughtful. "I've been working so hard lately," she mused. "I'm never around anymore. The girls are both so independent that I guess I've just assumed they didn't mind. But looking at them now—they just seem to be thriving on their grandparents' company!"

"That's different," Mr. Wakefield reminded her. "My parents are only out here for three weeks. They have a lot of catching up to do, remember."

"Still," Mrs. Wakefield said thoughtfully, "I do think I'm going to make an effort to get home earlier from now on. After all," she pointed out, "it won't be that long before the girls are in college. Look at Steve," she added.

The twins' older brother was a freshman at a nearby college, and there were stretches when he just couldn't get away from school.

Mr. Wakefield snapped his fingers. "I knew there was something I was supposed to tell you. Steve's coming home Saturday morning. He called me at the office today to tell me."

Mrs. Wakefield stared at him. "You see?" she said indignantly. "He didn't call *me*, did he?"

"He tried," Mr. Wakefield assured her. "You were in a meeting. Alice, it wasn't a big thing. It was only a phone call. He just felt bad because he wants to see more of his grandparents before they leave."

Mrs. Wakefield shook her head. "Even so," she said firmly, "I think I'm going to try to be around a lot more. I just get the impression I'm losing touch with my children."

"You could never lose touch," Mr. Wakefield said fondly, putting his hand on her arm. "You're the best mother in the whole world, Alice Wakefield. *And* the best wife. And don't you forget it!"

Mrs. Wakefield didn't answer. From the expression on her face, it was clear that Alice Wakefield hadn't been reassured by her husband's remarks.

But I'm going to do something about it, she told herself. *It's not too late to work at being a better mother!*

Four

Elizabeth was so engrossed in copy editing the article she had written that she barely heard the timid knock on the door of the *Oracle* office. "Emily!" she exclaimed, when the door opened and the petite brunette came inside. "I didn't expect to see you back here so soon! Don't tell me you've already finished your trial article."

Emily shook her head ruefully. "No way." She sighed. "Liz, I've spent hours poring over those old articles you gave me to read. But I might as well be reading Russian. I have no idea how to begin to write a story of my own!"

Elizabeth set down her note pad and swiveled in her chair to face Emily. "It isn't very easy at first," she admitted. "I remember the first story I did for *The Oracle*. It was a real bomb."

"How did you improve?" Emily asked, slipping out of her corduroy jacket and taking a seat at the table next to Elizabeth.

"Well, I guess I just practiced a lot. It's like anything else. The more comfortable you feel about what you're doing, the easier it gets."

"It's like playing the drums," Emily mused.

Elizabeth looked searchingly at the other girl. "Emily, are you sure you *want* to devote all this time to writing articles for the school paper? Wouldn't you rather be practicing the drums?"

"Liz," Emily said soberly, "I'm really getting frightened. Things at home are worse. I'm afraid if I don't do things the way Karen wants me to, I may have to leave Sweet Valley!"

Elizabeth pulled her ponytail to one side, as she often did when she was thinking hard. She wished she knew Emily Mayer well enough to tell her what she really thought. Because it was obvious to Elizabeth that the newspaper just wasn't the place for Emily's talents. She was a musician, not a writer. And she belonged with The Droids!

Besides, Elizabeth had little confidence that anyone, however dedicated, could transform herself the way Emily seemed to be hoping to do. The tried and true "be yourself" approach was the one that Elizabeth advocated. But she didn't feel she knew Emily well enough to say so. All she could do was listen. And the rest Emily would have to work out for herself.

To her surprise, Emily began to open up to her almost immediately. It was as if she'd been holding back so long that she couldn't stop herself once she began. She told Elizabeth all about Karen—and all about her father, too. How close they had been in the past and how strained things were between them now.

Elizabeth's heart went out to Emily. It was clear that she wasn't just paranoid about her stepmother. Karen sounded as if she were a confused woman, and she seemed to be taking things out on Emily.

But Elizabeth couldn't help feeling she hadn't heard the whole story yet. "Emily, I hate to ask a painful question," she said at last, "but how long ago did your mother die?"

Emily flushed hotly. "I—uh—" She fumbled with the edge of her spiral notebook for a minute or two before looking directly into Elizabeth's eyes. "Can you keep a secret?" she asked solemnly.

Elizabeth nodded.

"My mother isn't dead," Emily whispered. "That's just a story I made up. She isn't dead at all."

Elizabeth sat up straight in her chair. "But, Emily—why?" she asked softly. "Why would you say something like that?"

Emily stared at the floor. "Because," she said miserably, her face flaming, "I was embarrassed to tell anyone the truth. When I was seven years old, I came home from school one day and found out my mother had just taken off. She just"—tears filled Emily's eyes—"left a note on the kitchen counter—like she was going to the store or something. Only that wasn't what the note said. It said she was leaving and she wasn't coming back."

Elizabeth's heart skipped a beat. "You poor kid," she whispered, sliding from her chair to put her arm around Emily's trembling shoulders.

"It was pretty rough." Emily sighed. "She really meant it, too. She was in Chicago the next time I talked to her. And that's where she still is, as far as I know."

"You mean you haven't talked to her?" Elizabeth asked, horrified.

Emily blinked. "My mother isn't—well, she's not exactly a model mother, Liz. She has a lot of problems, from what I've heard. I feel like I know my mother's faults as well as I'd care to. She hurt me enough," she concluded bluntly. "All I want now is to live in peace."

"Wow." Elizabeth shook her head. "And now that Karen's giving you such a hard time, you can't really do that, can you?"

Emily shook her head. "I just don't know what's right anymore," she said nervously, getting up from her chair and pacing around the office. "Liz, I can't imagine leaving my home! It's all I've got, you know what I mean?"

Elizabeth nodded, a lump in her throat. She

felt horrible for Emily. It was almost impossible for her to imagine the kind of hurt and confusion Emily had experienced as a little girl. And now she was having to face all those painful feelings again. Much worse, she was being threatened with the loss of her father, the only family she really had. Not to mention her home, her school, and everything else that was familiar to her.

Elizabeth didn't know what to say. "I wish I could help somehow, Emily," she said. "Do you think there's anything I could do?"

"Just be my friend," Emily said impulsively, looking directly at Elizabeth. "And keep my secret for me, OK? I know it's kind of silly, but I just couldn't face anyone finding out about my mother. I don't know why I wanted to tell you, but I'm glad I did. I really feel like I can trust you," she concluded, looking away shyly.

"Of course I'll keep your secret," Elizabeth said warmly. "And I'm glad you told me, Emily. You can count on my friendship, no matter what."

"Thanks," Emily said gratefully, picking up her jacket. "You don't know how much that means to me, Liz."

"But I wouldn't worry too much about trying to work for the paper," Elizabeth advised her thoughtfully. "It sounds to me like you have enough on your mind. And if Karen can't accept you as you are, your problem isn't really solved at all by trying to change to please her."

"I think you're right about that," Emily admitted. "Besides," she said, giggling, "I'm really a terrible writer!"

"I'm sure that isn't true. But you're too talented musically to waste your time on something that doesn't really interest you."

"Liz," Emily said impulsively, "can I call you sometime if things at home get really bad? Or maybe come over? I just feel like things make so much more sense when I talk to you."

"Emily Mayer," Elizabeth exclaimed, "you are one-hundred-percent welcome in my house any time!"

Elizabeth was quiet for several minutes after Emily left the office. She had never heard a story quite as moving as the one Emily had just told her. She wished there were something she could do to help the girl. But she had a feeling the Mayers were going to have to work this out themselves.

She just hoped Emily would be strong enough to fight her own battle. Because if things went on this way much longer, Elizabeth thought grimly, Emily might not be able to stand the pressure. And there was no telling what might happen then.

"Chinese food!" Jessica shrieked, running into Elizabeth's room and jumping up and down.

"Do you realize," she added, calming herself long enough to grab her sister's hairbrush and position herself in front of the mirror over the dresser, "that we haven't been out for Chinese food in about six months?"

"Why do you suppose that is?" Elizabeth asked, tying a ribbon around her ponytail. "Do you think the fact that Dad can't stand it might have something to do with that?"

"I don't care," Jessica said happily, opening the top drawer of Elizabeth's dresser and extracting a silk scarf. "You weren't going to wear this tonight, were you?"

"I don't know," Elizabeth commented. "I can't get close enough to my dresser to decide *what* I'm going to wear." Actually, she was already dressed, but sometimes she liked to tease Jessica about her constant borrowing.

"Good," Jessica said sweetly, tying the scarf around her neck. "Grandma thinks I look nice with something blue next to my face. She says it makes my eyes bluer."

Elizabeth groaned. "Just make sure you don't get soy sauce all over it," she warned. "Do you think Mom will mind that we're going out?" she asked.

Jessica frowned at her reflection in the mirror, untying the scarf and refolding it. "Why should she mind? She'll probably be grateful that she and Dad can have a quiet evening together."

43

"I know," Elizabeth said thoughtfully, "but for the past day or two I've been getting the impression that—"

"Hey!" Mrs. Wakefield called cheerfully from the foot of the stairs. "Is anyone home? It's your long-lost mother, home early from the insane world of interior design!"

"Hi, Mom," Jessica called back, leaning closer to the mirror to inspect her eyes now that the scarf was retied around her throat.

"I am *so* happy to be home," Mrs. Wakefield continued, climbing up the stairs and entering Elizabeth's room. "Phew! I feel almost like a real person—getting home while it's still light outside."

"Did one of your clients cancel?" Elizabeth asked.

Mrs. Wakefield smiled. "Nope. As a matter of fact, I cancelled one of my clients. I suddenly got this incredible urge for an honest-to-goodness home-cooked meal—with all the frills. So I stopped at the market on the way home and picked up six of the biggest, juiciest steaks you've ever seen. And I got baking potatoes and sour cream and everything we need for a wonderful salad."

Jessica and Elizabeth exchanged uneasy glances. "Uh, Mom, we sort of—" Elizabeth began.

"We're going out for Chinese food tonight," Jessica interrupted. "Grandma and Grandpa say there's one of the best Cantonese restaurants in the whole country about half an hour from here. And we thought—"

"We had no idea you were planning to cook a big dinner," Elizabeth said.

"Oh," Mrs. Wakefield said, crestfallen. "Oh, well."

"Can you keep the steaks?" Jessica asked. "We could have a cook-out tomorrow."

Mrs. Wakefield thought for a minute. "Maybe we could *all* go out tonight," she ventured hopefully. "I haven't gotten a chance to see much of you two lately, and that way maybe—"

"Mom," Jessica said pointedly, "Dad doesn't like Chinese food, remember? He says it makes him sick."

"Well, we could go to a different kind of restaurant," Mrs. Wakefield tried again.

Jessica looked anguished. "Mom, we've been planning this for *ages*! We can't change our plans now, anyway," she added. "It would absolutely *crush* Grandma Wakefield."

"I see," Mrs. Wakefield said. "Well, some other time," she said vaguely, stepping out into the hallway.

"Jessica," Elizabeth said anxiously after their mother had left, "do you think she minded? We could always ask Grandma and Grandpa to make it some other night."

"Don't be silly," Jessica hissed. "Anyway," she added, giving her hair a final once-over with Elizabeth's brush, "mothers don't get insecure about things like this, Liz. And Mom would tell us if she really minded!"

"I guess you're right," Elizabeth agreed, flipping off the light switch.

Still, it looked as though something was bothering their mother, Elizabeth thought as she followed her twin from the room. But Jessica was right—it couldn't possibly be something as silly as a Chinese dinner. And whatever it was, Elizabeth was sure their mother would tell them if it was something really important.

Emily had come home from her talk with Elizabeth determined to make a fresh start. *Liz is right*, she told herself resolutely. *There's no point in trying to win Karen over by trying to be someone I'm not. If Karen wants a writer in the family, she'll just have to wait till Karrie is old enough!*

But any optimism she felt walking home disappeared as soon as Emily walked through the front door. Or at least as soon as she riffled through the mail on the kitchen counter and found three brochures from boarding schools in New England. *Boy*, Emily thought, taking a deep breath. *Karen really means business!*

She felt better, though, the minute she closed the door to the basement and went down to the studio her father had helped her build. This was Emily's favorite room, and it was entirely her own. Together Emily and her father had walled off a large corner of the basement and set up her drums there. Everything Emily loved best was in her studio. She kept all her sheet music in a big chest in the corner. And there was a big, comfortable chair to sit in when she wasn't playing. Sometimes she just went down there to think.

More and more, in fact. Because Karen had very strict rules about when Emily was allowed to practice. *But now's one of the times I'm allowed to*, Emily thought, checking her watch. Karrie never slept between four and six.

Besides, Emily had been waiting for this moment all day. She had ordered a new set of cymbals from a music store in Los Angeles, and they had been delivered the previous day! Emily still hadn't had a chance to try them out because Karrie had been asleep and Karen refused to let Emily so much as tap the cymbal with the stick to see how it sounded.

Well, the cymbals were all set up, and Emily was ready to go. Within minutes she had forgotten everything but the rhythm of the music as she turned on her cassette recorder and began hitting the drums with her drumsticks. There was something about the rhythm of a good song that just pulled Emily in, until it seemed as if her entire soul were made of music.

She was lost in the sound of the new cymbals when Karen opened the door to the studio. "Emily!" Karen yelled, her eyes flashing angrily. "I have *finally* gotten Karrie to fall asleep, and now you've gone and woken her up again!"

Emily stared at her stepmother. "But we agreed that between four o'clock and—"

"I don't care *what* we agreed," Karen said acidly. "I have absolutely had it with this constant noise, young lady. If you simply refuse to cooperate with a few simple rules—"

"But I'm *not* refusing!" Emily cried. "You just keep changing the rules on me all the time! Karen, I can't just—"

If the phone hadn't run at that moment, Emily knew she would have broken down entirely. But the sharp peal of the phone temporarily broke the angry tension that hung between them. "I'll get it," Emily said quickly, hurrying for the extension that her father had had installed in the adjoining family room.

It was Dan.

"It's for me," Emily said, covering the receiver with her hand and looking quizzically at Karen, who had followed her. "Do you want me to call back, or—"

Karen's face darkened with anger. "Oh, do what you please," she said, heading for the stairs. "Just make sure you cut out the noise. Because the next time you bother little Karrie—I mean it, Emily, the *next* time . . ." Her voice trailed off, and the warning hung in the air.

"I can't make practice tonight," she told Dan, fighting back the tears. She hadn't told him anything about her problems at home, and she felt too upset to make up a good excuse. But she was certain that breaking curfew that night wouldn't be a good idea. Not with Karen on the rampage.

"I want to hear your new cymbals," Dan complained. "Why don't I come over? I could come tomorrow after school."

Emily thought fast. She would love to show Dan her private studio. But Karen . . .

Suddenly Emily remembered that Karen was taking Karrie to the doctor the following afternoon. If they timed it right, she didn't see any reason that Karen had to find out.

"That's a good idea," Emily said warmly, twisting the phone cord between her fingers. "Why don't you meet me after last period under the clock at school? We can come back here together."

"Great," Dan said. "What shall I tell everyone at practice tonight?" he added.

Emily sighed. "Tell them I'm still sick," she said. "That'll just have to do for now."

But I'm taking a big risk, she thought unhappily. Dana, for one, was going to begin to wonder why Emily was always fine at school but kept getting sick in the evenings.

Emily couldn't see any way out of the mess she was in. The Droids was one thing. She was beginning to face the fact that she might not be able to stay in the band—not if she wanted to stay in Sweet Valley, too.

But Dan . . . Dan was different. Emily wasn't going to risk losing his friendship.

Five

"Jessica," Elizabeth said thoughtfully, rolling over on her stomach to reach for the suntan lotion next to the striped towel she'd spread on the grass, "have you noticed anything strange about the way Mom's been behaving, or am I imagining things?"

"Mmm," Jessica said sleepily, opening one eye to contemplate her sister. "What are you talking about?"

"Well, haven't you noticed how strange she's been acting?" Elizabeth pointed out. "Jessica, she must have asked us to do things with her about five times in the last two days. I don't know what's going on, but all of a sudden she really seems to want our company."

"I think you're imagining it," Jessica said. "Face it, Liz, you're just a worrier."

"OK," Elizabeth said, ticking things off on her fingers. "To begin with there was dinner

51

last night. No matter what you say, I think she was really upset about it. Didn't you notice how quiet she was when we got back?"

"Mmm," Jessica murmured.

"And *then*," Elizabeth said, counting off the second finger, "she wanted to take us to a movie! That was so weird—especially since Grandma had just suggested going out for a walk."

"You haven't convinced me yet." Jessica yawned.

"OK," Elizabeth said. "What about today, then? Calling us up from the office to see if she could take us for a drive along the beach? Does that seem normal to you?"

"No," Jessica agreed. "It doesn't. Thank goodness we got out of it," she said. "If Grandma and Grandpa hadn't already promised to take us shopping at Hampshire Place, we might've had to go!"

Elizabeth couldn't help feeling that Jessica was wrong about their mother. "I just don't get it. Is there something we've done that's made her feel strange?"

"I wouldn't worry about it," Jessica said. "You should read this book Lila showed me the other day on meditation, Liz. You really seem like the type who needs it."

Elizabeth groaned. "I need it like a hole in the head," she grumbled. "No, Jess, I really think—"

Jessica sat straight up, cocking her ear. "Did

52

you just hear the phone ring?" she demanded, her expression intent.

Elizabeth burst out laughing. She hadn't heard a thing, but she often thought her twin had a special sixth sense when it came to the telephone or the door bell ringing.

"It *is* ringing!" Jessica exclaimed. She streaked across the lawn for the back door as if her life depended on getting to the phone before whoever was calling hung up.

"Liz, it's for you," Jessica called out the kitchen window.

Elizabeth walked into the house. "Emily Mayer," Jessica told her, covering the receiver with her hand. "*Now* you have something to worry about," she added, shaking her head as she passed her sister the phone. "She said something absolutely awful happened, and she has to talk to you right away!"

Emily still couldn't believe the chain of events that had taken place that afternoon.

She and Dan had met after their last class, as they'd planned. They had walked the mile and a half to Emily's house, and it was one of the most pleasant times Emily could remember in ages. Dan was such a nice person, she found herself thinking. There were a number of things about him that appealed to her: his sharp wit, an unusual sensitivity about music, and the fact that he knew a lot about a good many things, including, it turned out, science. Dan really wanted to study physics one day. He was telling Emily about the connection between music and physics when they reached the Mayers' house. No one was home, as Emily had expected, so she opened the front door with her house key.

Emily had been slightly nervous at first about being alone in the house with a guy she didn't know very well. But Dan made her feel comfortable right away. In fact, before she knew it, they were talking as if they were best friends. Dan kept making her laugh so hard she almost cried over his descriptions of the people in a band he used to play with.

She couldn't remember the last time she'd laughed like that. In fact, Emily simply couldn't remember the last time she'd felt so relaxed. And just as she'd predicted, it was wonderful showing Dan her studio. She could tell he liked it as much as she did.

Naturally Dan had wanted to hear her new cymbals. The next thing Emily knew she was playing her heart out, playing in a way she hadn't for months.

She was so engrossed in the music that she didn't hear the garage door open upstairs—or the door slam as Karen came in. She didn't even hear little Karrie crying. The next thing she knew Karen was downstairs, the sobbing baby in her arms. Karen's pretty face was contorted with rage as she stared first at Emily and then at Dan.

"I thought I made myself clear yesterday, Emily," she seethed, trying her best to quiet Karrie. "Did I or didn't I tell you that there is to be no more noise in this house?"

Emily felt the color draining from her face. *Not in front of Dan,* she thought desperately. *Please, Karen, don't humiliate me this way!*

But Karen was just getting started. "I'm afraid you haven't introduced me to your friend," she said acidly, turning to look at Dan. The way she said "friend" sounded so awful that Emily cringed.

"I'm Dan Scott," Dan managed. "I think maybe I'd better be going now."

"Yes," Karen said furiously, "I think maybe you'd better! Emily," she added, her face burning, "since when do you invite boys over without asking my permission? Since when do you invite boys into the house when no one else is home?"

Emily felt sick. "I—uh—"

"*You* may not care how it looks to other people," Karen went on, "but once again, young lady, you don't have just yourself to think of anymore."

Emily felt angry tears stinging her eyes. "We weren't doing anything wrong, Karen," she protested. "You can see for yourself. I was just showing Dan my new cymbals! I wasn't—"

"Don't tell me what you were or weren't doing," Karen fumed. "I've warned your father a million times," she added. "Why do you think I set curfews for you? Don't you understand it's just to keep this sort of thing from happening? Believe me," she added, her voice rising, "I know what kind of home you were raised in, Emily. I know your own mother didn't care about things like curfews before she walked out on your father! But I"—her voice dropped—"am *not* going to permit you to turn out like your mother. Among other things, I simply will *not* have my baby grow up in a house with a—a tramp!"

At the mention of her mother, Emily had frozen. She barely heard the words that followed. All she knew was that her secret had been given away. Dan knew now that she was a liar, that her mother was still alive. And worse, he knew what people thought of her mother. *Tramp.* That was the word Karen had used, and that was the word Emily had heard from time to time when she was a little girl.

And Dan also knew how little her stepmother thought of her—how horribly she treated her.

Well, it didn't matter anymore. Nothing mattered anymore. Dan knew everything there was to know, and all Emily wanted was for him to leave the house as soon as possible. She never wanted to see him again. Now that he knew what she really was, what her mother was . . .

"I think I'd better leave," Dan repeated. Karen had burst into tears, and little Karrie was crying, too. Emily was too numb to cry.

She barely looked at Dan as he left. She didn't ever want to look him in the eyes again, she realized. She didn't think she could bear it. Not after what he'd just heard.

But within minutes tears had welled up in Emily's eyes. Karen had run upstairs, still crying, with Karrie in her arms. And Emily was left alone.

Almost without thinking, she reached for the telephone. "Call me any time you need me," Elizabeth Wakefield had said.

Well, this is as good a time as any, Emily thought. She certainly couldn't remember a time in her life when things had seemed worse—or when she had felt more devastatingly and utterly alone.

Six

Emily shivered. It was chilly out, and in her haste she had forgotten her jacket. But then she really hadn't been thinking straight when she'd left the house. She'd just wanted to get out—fast.

Emily had talked to Elizabeth for less than a minute before she broke down. Tears streaming down her face, she had tried to tell Elizabeth what had happened. But she knew she wasn't making sense.

"Can you come over?" Elizabeth asked her. "You sound terrible, Emily. Why don't you come over right away, and we can talk about whatever it is that happened?"

"OK," Emily had told her. "But don't worry if it takes me a little while to get over to your house," she'd added. "I think I'm going to walk. It helps me to calm down."

It felt strange to Emily to have confided in Elizabeth Wakefield. Up until a week ago, Eliz-

59

abeth had been no more than a casual acquaintance—the sort of girl Emily wished she knew better but never felt entirely comfortable with. She had always thought of Elizabeth as a girl who had everything—good looks, a great sense of humor, outstanding grades, and a wonderful family.

For those reasons, Emily could never have imagined dumping her own problems on Elizabeth. It was as if all the qualities that made Elizabeth so admirable also made her seem unapproachable.

But the minute Elizabeth began to talk to her the other afternoon at the *Oracle* office, Emily had warmed to her. Elizabeth might well be the girl who had everything, but everything included being sympathetic and warm. And Emily could tell that she cared. She wasn't just pretending to listen. Everything about her was genuine.

In a funny way it was easier for Emily to confide in Elizabeth than in any of her old friends, such as Dana Larson. The other members of The Droids—Guy Chesney, who played keyboards and Max Dellon, who played the guitar—had known Emily for ages. They joked around a lot and often ate lunch together at school. But Emily could never have confided in any of them—not even Dana. The atmosphere of the band was low-key, almost lighthearted. It was almost as if there were an unwritten rule against getting serious about anything. Emily had tried on several occasions to talk to Dana about Karen, but she always felt as if she were turning down a dead-end street the minute the conversation became serious. Dana just didn't seem ready to talk about Emily's personal problems.

As for Dan, Emily couldn't even bring herself to think about him without feeling her cheeks burn as she relived that terrible scene that afternoon. A few hours earlier she might have thought she could confide in Dan. She had really begun to like him a lot.

Well, all that's over now, Emily thought, kicking a stone out of her path. *What's going to happen to me?* she wondered, a lump forming in her throat. How could she go back and act as if everything were normal after all those horrible things Karen had said to her?

But Emily didn't know what other choice she had. She didn't know where else she could go.

Tears filled Emily's eyes as Karen's words rang again in her memory. "I am not going to permit you to turn out like your mother!" Karen had said. "I simply will not have my baby grow up in a house with a tramp!"

A tramp, Emily thought dully. *That's what my mother turned out to be. Who's to say I haven't already started to take after her? Maybe I don't have any choice.*

But Emily knew in her heart she didn't believe that. She knew Karen had been wrong to shout those horrible things at her—especially in front of Dan.

Moreover, she knew she had to do something fast. She had tried to talk to her father on numerous occasions, and it hadn't helped. One way or another, something was going to have to give. She prayed that Elizabeth would have some good ideas. The way things were, the whole fabric of her life was unraveling before her eyes. Her home, her family, her friends—everything seemed to be falling apart.

And she was running out of strength. Unless Elizabeth could help somehow, Emily had no idea what she was going to do.

The Wakefields had just sat down at the dining-room table when the door bell rang.

"I'll get it," Elizabeth said, jumping to her feet. "That must be Emily Mayer."

"Emily Mayer?" Mr. Wakefield echoed quizzically, wiping his mouth with his napkin and looking questioningly at Mrs. Wakefield across the table. "Who's Emily Mayer?"

"She's in our class at school," Jessica said. "And I think she's having some problems at home," she added in a stage whisper.

"Oh, dear," Grandma Wakefield said, looking distraught. "That sort of thing upsets me so much. I just don't know what's happening to the American family these days."

"Parents don't have enough time for their

children any more, that's what it is," Grandpa Wakefield said. "Alice, this steak is delicious," he added appreciatively. "Did you add something special to it, or is it just the air out here that makes it taste so good?"

Mrs. Wakefield was looking distractedly at Jessica and apparently didn't hear what her father-in-law had said. "Jess, do you ever feel that I don't have enough time for you and Liz? I mean—"

"Shhh," Jessica said. "They're coming in here, Mom!"

"I'd like to introduce you all to Emily Mayer," Elizabeth said, drawing the brunette into the dining room. "Emily, this is the Wakefield clan! You already know Jessica, and this is my mother, my father, and my grandparents, who're visiting from Michigan."

"Nice to meet you," Emily murmured, looking around the crowded table and forcing herself to smile.

"Emily, pull up a chair," Mr. Wakefield said warmly, getting up from the table and fitting a seat between Elizabeth and her grandmother. "Would you like something to eat?"

Emily shook her head. "No, thanks, I'm not very hungry," she said, taking the seat he offered her.

"Food," Grandma Wakefield said quickly, "is absolutely crucial for all growing girls. Alice, let me get this girl a plate so she can have some steak."

"I'll get it," Mrs. Wakefield said weakly, trying to catch her husband's eye.

"We can talk later," Elizabeth murmured to Emily when her mother had left the room. "I know you don't want to go into the whole thing now, with all these people around."

Emily shrugged. "I really can't hide the truth much longer," she said. "In fact, I came over here because I wanted to ask you if I could stay here for a little while."

The table went perfectly quiet. "You mean stay here, in our house?" Mr. Wakefield asked gently, looking searchingly at Emily. "Are you in some kind of trouble?"

In the next instant Emily burst into tears.

"You poor, poor thing!" Grandma Wakefield exclaimed, leaping up to throw her arms around Emily just as Mrs. Wakefield was trying to set a plate down in front of her. They collided, and the plate flew out of Mrs. Wakefield's hands, breaking into several pieces on the floor.

"Alice, I'm so sorry!" Grandma Wakefield said, a look of consternation on her face.

"It's all right," Mrs. Wakefield said, looking too drained to care. "Liz, can you get another plate from the kitchen? And the dustpan?"

"It's all my fault," Emily insisted, brushing the tears from her eyes. "I make a mess out of everything these days."

"Emily," Mr. Wakefield said calmly, "why don't we take this all one step at a time? Can you tell us exactly what's wrong at home?"

Emily took a long, quavering breath. "OK," she said. "But it's kind of a long story."

For the next ten minutes there was absolute silence from the Wakefields. No one said a word but Emily. Occasionally her voice would trail off as she came to a particularly difficult part of the story. It wasn't easy to tell everyone about her mother or about the problems she'd been having with Karen.

But Emily could tell that everyone wanted to help her. And she was certain her only chance now was to tell them everything. If they were going to help her, they had to know the truth.

When she described what had taken place that afternoon, Emily almost broke down. "It was so embarrassing," she said softly, her eyes shining with tears. "I mean, it would have been bad enough to have to listen to all that stuff about my mother by myself! But having Dan there, knowing what he must think of me now. . ."

"I'm sure he understands," Elizabeth said gently, putting her hand on Emily's arm.

Emily shook her head. "I came here because I didn't know what else to do," she concluded in a low voice. "My father is going to take Karen's side again. I just know it! And I can't stay there anymore with things the way they're going. I just can't."

Mr. Wakefield sighed and looked across the table at his wife. "This is a pretty delicate situation, Emily," he said gently. "We want to do everything we can to help you, but I'm afraid we'd be overstepping our bounds, morally *and* legally, if we tried to take matters into our own hands. Do you understand?"

"Are you saying you won't help?" Emily demanded, her shoulders beginning to shake.

"We want to help," Mrs. Wakefield told her, leaning forward in her chair. "But we need to know first what you want us to do."

"Let me stay here for a while," Emily begged. "Just until I figure out something to do! Please," she added desperately, staring pleadingly at Mr. Wakefield. "I don't know what I'll do if you say no!"

Mr. Wakefield sighed deeply. "You can certainly stay here tonight," he said at last, lifting his eyebrows questioningly at Mrs. Wakefield and seeing by her small nod that she had no objection. "Maybe that will help everyone cool off a little. But we can only let you stay here on one condition," he added.

"What's that?" Emily asked, her voice breaking a little.

"You'll have to call your father right after dinner and tell him where you are, that you're safe, and that you'll be staying here tonight. Otherwise, he'll be out of his mind with worry."

Emily stared down at her lap. She had been so nervous that she'd torn her napkin into little pieces without even realizing what she was doing.

One night wasn't quite what she'd hoped for, but it was better than nothing. Emily wasn't that sure her father even cared where she was at this point, but she could see that Mr. Wakefield was right. "OK," she said finally, biting her lip, "I'll call him."

"Now, *eat!*" Grandma Wakefield exclaimed, passing her the breadbasket. "No wonder you're so upset! You probably haven't eaten a thing all day, you poor skinny child!"

Everyone laughed, and the tension in the room was at least partly dissolved.

But Emily could barely swallow the delicious food the twins' grandmother placed before her. All she could think about was the phone call she'd promised to make when dinner was over. What would her father say?

When Emily was little, before her mother had left, she would invent pleasant scenarios to dwell on when she was upset, little daydreams of the best thing that could possibly happen. Now she found herself doing the same thing. Maybe Karen would tell her father that she was sorry, Emily thought. Maybe when Emily called, he would say he was sorry, too. And then they'd say they were on their way over to pick her up.

"Have a potato, Emily," Grandpa Wakefield instructed, and Emily's daydream dissolved. She was back in reality, and the dreaded phone call was getting closer every minute.

"Emily?" Her father's voice sounded strained. "Where are you?" he asked. Emily couldn't tell by his tone whether he was angry or not.

"I'm at a friend's house," she said, checking over her shoulder to make sure the door to the study was still closed.

"Which friend?" her father asked. "Are you at the Larsons'?"

Emily didn't answer. "Daddy, about this afternoon . . ." she began, nervously twisting the telephone cord.

"I heard all about it," her father said shortly. "And to tell you the truth, Emily, I've just about had it. If you can't learn to get along with Karen, I just don't know what I'm going to do with you! Didn't I ask you to try to be more cooperative? You just can't go banging around on those drums with a baby in the house!"

Emily felt her eyes fill with tears. "Banging around on those drums"—that was the way her father was describing the thing that meant most in the whole world to her!

"I wasn't just 'banging around,' " Emily said furiously. "I was showing Dan my new cymbals. And Karen was out, Daddy! She'd taken Karrie to the doctor's, and I was completely alone!"

"Another sore point," her father told her. "Karen has asked you to observe some very simple rules about curfews and having friends over without a chaperon. And you refuse to follow them."

"Daddy," Emily said, her throat aching, "did Karen tell you what she said about Mom?"

"No," Mr. Mayer said abruptly. "What are you talking about, Em?"

Emily couldn't answer. Of course Karen hadn't told him, she thought miserably. She'd never make herself look bad.

But Emily couldn't bring herself to repeat Karen's words to her father. It would hurt him terribly. And she had a feeling it wouldn't do much good anyway. She was beginning to realize that she was fighting a losing battle.

"I don't want to talk about this over the phone," her father told her. "Now, if you'll just tell me where you are, I'll come over and get you, Em. Cut the dramatic stuff and let me know where you are."

Emily sighed. "I'm not coming home, Dad."

"What?" Mr. Mayer demanded. "Emily, I'm not playing games. Now, tell me where you are!"

"I'm not playing games either," Emily said, shocked by how cold her voice sounded. "I can't live the way I've been living anymore, Daddy. And I'm not coming home."

"Emily," her father said, pronouncing her name as if it hurt him, "if you're not back in this house in exactly one hour, I'm going to put your drums out on the street. Do you understand me?"

Emily gasped. "You wouldn't do that!" she cried. The silence on the other end of the phone told her she was wrong. *This can't be happening,* she thought dully, staring at the receiver.

"OK," she said abruptly, not stopping to think. "I'll be home as soon as I can."

"What happened?" Elizabeth asked with concern when Emily opened the door to the study.

"I have to go home," Emily said. Suddenly she realized how tired she was. Her body ached all over, and even her eyes seemed to be sore.

"Is everything OK?" Elizabeth asked, putting her arm around Emily.

The other girl took a deep breath. "I don't know," she said at last. "But I have to go home."

"We'll come with you," Jessica said, hurrying over to the front hall closet to get her jacket. "We can give you a ride."

"Why don't you let me—" Mrs. Wakefield began.

But Grandpa Wakefield cut her off. "We'll drive," he said firmly. "That way we can keep the twins company on the way back. We'll take Ned's car."

Mrs. Wakefield opened her mouth to object, but the next thing she knew, Jessica had thrown her arms around her grandfather, kissing him on the cheek.

"You're the best grandfather in the whole world," Jessica said.

And Mrs. Wakefield felt as though she could sympathize when Emily's eyes filled with wistful tears. Emily Mayer wasn't the only one who felt like a stranger in her own family, Mrs. Wakefield thought unhappily. Now more than ever she was sure she'd lost touch with the twins. But what could she do to regain their love?

Seven

"Emily!" Dan called, hurrying through the hall. The second bell had just rung, and students were crowding the main corridor, hurrying to their next classes. Dan was sure Emily had seen him, but she didn't slow down. She didn't turn around when he called her name, either.

Emily had been on Dan's mind every minute since he'd left her house the day before. In fact, he'd telephoned her house three times, but he couldn't get through. The first time her father had told him she wasn't home. He had sounded upset. The second time, the phone had been busy. And the third time, Emily's stepmother had answered the phone. "Emily can't talk now," she had said curtly. She hadn't asked him if he wanted to leave a message.

Dan had never experienced anything like what had taken place the previous day in Emily's studio. Not that he didn't occasionally have arguments with his mother. Everyone did. But what he had witnessed in the Mayers' basement wasn't just an argument. He had never met Emily's stepmother before, and maybe it wasn't fair to judge her solely by the way she'd behaved then, but Dan felt furious every time he thought about the way she'd screamed at Emily. He felt helpless, too. He wished there were some way he could help Emily. From the small dose he'd tasted, her stepmother seemed like strong medicine.

And the way she'd talked about Emily's mother . . . Dan didn't know the real story behind all that. He didn't care, either. Dana had told him that Emily's mother had died when she was really little. But the way her stepmother was talking, it sounded as though she were still alive. Dan shuddered every time he thought of it.

It would have made him angry to hear someone talk that way to any of his close friends. But Emily—well, Emily was special. Dan had always liked her, but he'd been too shy to let her know how much he cared. The truth was that he cared a great deal. He even kept a picture of her in his desk drawer at home. It was a picture of all The Droids, actually, which had been taken at a school dance and published in *The Oracle*. You couldn't see any of them all that well, but Emily had come out best. She was so pretty, Dan thought. So tiny—almost delicate looking. And she was smart and sensitive. It infuriated him to think of anyone hurting her.

Dan didn't know exactly what he could do to help. But he felt that he had to talk to her, had to let her know that he was behind her, no matter what.

"Emily, wait up!" he cried, running to catch up with her before she turned the corner.

"What is it?" Emily asked, turning to stare at him.

Dan was taken aback by the look on her face. He hadn't known exactly what to expect from her, whether she'd be embarrassed or upset or just try to pretend nothing had happened. But he hadn't expected her to look so cold!

"I need to talk to you," Dan said urgently, putting his hand on her arm. "Em, what happened yesterday really upset me. Can we just—"

"What happened yesterday," Emily said coolly, pulling away from him, "is absolutely fine now, Dan. I'm sorry you had to be involved. But everything's fine."

Dan stared at her. "But, Emily, your stepmother said—"

"My stepmother was just kind of upset," Emily told him. "She shouldn't have said all that stuff in front of you. She really feels bad about it."

"But what about—" What about *us*? Dan wanted to ask. But Emily was acting so strangely he was afraid to say anything like that. "What about your new cymbals?" he asked lamely.

Emily shook her head. "I think I'm through with my new cymbals," she told him. "As a matter of fact, Dan, I might as well tell you this now, since you've brought it up. I'm quitting The Droids."

Dan felt as if he'd had the wind knocked out of him. "You can't do that!" he exclaimed. "Emily, The Droids are the best band in Sweet Valley! Playing with them is such a great opportunity! Besides," he added, his face falling, "what are we going to do without you? You're so talented, Em. You can't just—"

"Dan," Emily said, her voice completely emotionless, "I've thought this over very carefully. And I'm through. I guess it was sort of a phase I went through," she added, staring past Dan. "But in any case, I'm sick and tired of the whole thing now. Besides, Karen really needs my help around the house these days. And I intend to be around when she needs me."

Here goes nothing, Dan thought. *If I don't say something now, I may never get the chance again.*

"What about us?" he asked, his mouth dry. "Emily, I've never told you this before, but I really—"

For a second, Dan thought that Emily was going to burst into tears. Her expression flickered slightly, and she looked as if she were going to reach out and hang onto him for dear life.

But the next minute she was back in control. "Dan, I have to run," she said quickly. And that was it. She just turned away and hurried down the hall, leaving him standing there.

Dan was dumbstruck. He couldn't believe Emily was serious about leaving The Droids.

And why was she talking about trying to help out her stepmother—when it was obvious from what had happened the previous day that they despised each other?

Emily's behavior struck Dan as peculiar. He couldn't help feeling that she was trying desperately to maintain control, that if she dropped her act even for one second, she'd crumble.

I've got to do something, he thought anxiously. *I just have to.*

But what could he possibly do to help her?

"Liz, can I talk to you for a minute?" Emily asked, sticking her head inside the door to the *Oracle* office.

"Come on in," Elizabeth said. "I've been trying to find you all day!"

"Don't worry," Emily said promptly, avoiding Elizabeth's searching gaze. "Everything's fine, just fine."

Elizabeth stared at her. "What do you mean? What did Karen say when you got in? Did she apologize?"

Emily took a deep breath. "We had a really long talk, all three of us," she began. "And I think everything's going to be OK now, Liz. To be honest, I really don't feel like talking about it anymore."

Elizabeth felt something was still very wrong. "So you guys figured out some reasonable way to work things out?" she asked doubtfully.

"Well," Emily said, averting her eyes, "I could sort of see where Karen was coming from a little better last night. I guess I haven't been very easy to deal with. And that's one reason why I wanted to talk to you, Liz. I want to run an ad in next week's *Oracle*. Can you tell me how to do it?"

"Sure," Elizabeth said. "Are you selling something?"

Emily lowered her eyes. "My drums."

Elizabeth stared at her. "Your . . . Emily, are you kidding?"

"No," Emily said flatly. "I'm not."

"But why would you want to sell your drums? Emily, you're the best drummer in the whole school! What's going to happen to The Droids without you?"

"There are lots of drummers," Emily said in a low tone. "I wasn't that good, Liz. Besides, it doesn't mean that much to me anymore."

Elizabeth stared at Emily, a terrible thought dawning on her. "Emily, did you and your parents talk more about boarding school last night? Does that have anything to do with your decision to give up the drums?"

Emily's face reddened. "I don't want to talk about it."

"Just tell me one thing," Elizabeth demanded. "Did you make some sort of deal with your stepmother? Did you promise to give up your drums so you wouldn't be sent away from Sweet Valley?"

Emily unfolded a small square of paper. "Look," she said, her voice trembling. "Here's the ad I want to run. Just put it in the paper for me, Liz, and let me know how much it costs."

Elizabeth took the piece of paper, which looked as though it had been folded and unfolded dozens of times. "Em," she began again, pleadingly. But when she looked up, Emily was gone.

She looked down at the paper again. It read:

For Sale: One Set of Drums and Cymbals,
　Excellent Condition
　$200.00 or Best Offer

Elizabeth shook her head. *I can't let her do it,* she thought grimly. She was practically sure that her hunch was right, that Karen had threatened to send Emily away if she didn't play by her rules.

Elizabeth didn't blame Emily. If that were the choice, she herself would probably do the same thing, she thought sympathetically. But she also knew how terribly unhappy Emily must be. Quitting The Droids seemed to be the very worst thing she could do.

"Dan!" Elizabeth exclaimed. It was after school, and the corridor was almost deserted. Dan Scott was one of the few other students around. "I've been hoping I'd run into you today," Elizabeth confided as Dan strolled over to her locker. "I wanted to talk to you about Emily. She told me what happened after school yesterday," Elizabeth said. "That must have been terrible for both of you."

"It was awkward for me," Dan said, leaning against the locker next to Elizabeth's and staring at the floor. "God knows what it must have been like for poor Emily. It's . . . well, to be honest, it's kind of hard to tell exactly what she's feeling about things right now. I think she's trying to convince herself everything's OK. But I don't buy it."

"Me, neither," Elizabeth said. "Has she talked to you about quitting The Droids?"

Dan nodded. "It's crazy," he said vehemently. "Not just because we'd be losing such a good drummer, either. But I know how much music means to her. Emily could really make it if she keeps it up!"

"I don't know if I should tell you this or not." Elizabeth hesitated, then continued. "She brought me an ad this afternoon that she wants to run in the school paper. She wants to sell her drums."

Dan slapped his forehead. "She's crazy!" he cried. "How much is she asking for them?" he added a moment later.

"I don't know." Elizabeth tried to remember. "Two hundred dollars, I think."

Dan shook his head. "That crazy kid. Those drums are worth a lot more than that. And Emily probably saved up all her life for them. Elizabeth, if she really runs that ad, someone might actually buy them! And then she'll never be able to change her mind!"

"I know," Elizabeth said. "And I'm sure she's going to regret it. It sounds to me as if her stepmother has given her some kind of ultimatum. I tried to talk to her about it, but she wouldn't open up to me at all."

"She treated me as if I were a complete stranger," Dan muttered, sticking his hands in his pockets.

Elizabeth stared searchingly up into Dan's face. It sounded to her as if this was more than just a case of professional sympathy.

"She's pretty upset," Elizabeth said gently. "If I were you, I'd hang in there, Dan."

Dan blushed a deep red. "I don't have any choice," he said in a low voice. "Not feeling the way I do."

"Look," Elizabeth said desperately, "isn't there anything we can do? I thought about sort of accidentally losing her ad or just forgetting to print it, but she'll see that it isn't in the paper next week and want to know why."

"Well," Dan said slowly, rocking back and forth a little on his heels, "maybe you should just go ahead and print it. It doesn't seem as though you have much choice. After all," he added, a shy smile breaking across his face, "it would be unethical not to do what Emily asked you to do."

"But if I run it," Elizabeth argued, "someone might just go ahead and buy her drums!"

Dan's smile broadened. "Yes," he agreed. "In fact, I have a pretty strong hunch someone *will* buy them."

"But—" Elizabeth stared at him. Suddenly she began to smile. "I get it," she said. "You mean . . ."

"Run the ad," Dan told her, giving her a conspiratorial wink. "Who knows," he added, half to himself. "A set of drums like that for two hundred dollars—why, I might be interested myself!"

Elizabeth burst out laughing. Suddenly she felt a little better about Emily Mayer. It was good to know that she herself wasn't the only one who had the girl's best interests at heart!

Eight

It was Saturday morning a week later, and Emily was in Karrie's nursery, playing with her. "You see," she murmured, running her hand tenderly through the soft blond locks on Karrie's head, "this isn't so bad, is it? I'm doing OK so far, right, Karrie?"

Karrie stared up at her, stuffing her fist in her mouth. Smiling widely, she made one of the little noises that her mother insisted was "talking." Emily sighed. What a beautiful little baby, she thought.

It almost hurt Emily to look at Karrie sometimes. She was so incredibly delicate—so vulnerable. She was a sweet, contented baby, Emily thought, still stroking the child's hair. She didn't know how much unhappiness there was in the world.

I used to be just like this, Emily thought. *I was a little baby, too. And maybe my mother picked me up the way Karen picks up little Karrie. Maybe she worried when I couldn't sleep. Maybe . . .*

Tears stung Emily's eyes. "I want to protect you!" she said, picking Karrie up and holding her tightly. "I wish I could keep you from ever finding out what a mess things really are around here!"

Karrie made a soft cooing noise, her wide blue eyes fixed on Emily's face.

"Emily," Karen said, coming into the nursery, "the phone just rang. Didn't you hear it?"

Emily shook her head, putting little Karrie in her crib. "Sorry," she said, trying to keep her voice even. "Is it for me?"

"Yes," Karen said, not looking one bit pleased. "It's that boy again—the one who was over here the other day."

Emily took a deep breath as she brushed past her stepmother. It was *impossible* to please her, Emily thought.

Emily picked up the extension in her bedroom. "Hi, Dan," she said. "What's up?"

"I just wanted to see how you're doing," Dan said cheerfully. "We really missed you at practice last week, Em. We're all hoping that you'll change your—"

"Dan, I don't want to talk about The Droids," Emily said shortly. "If that's why you called—"

"Well," Dan said quickly, "as a matter of fact, that isn't why I called, Emily. I saw your ad in *The Oracle*. Are you serious about selling your drums?"

Emily took a deep breath. "Yes," she said. "And don't try to talk me out of it, either! I know what I'm doing, Dan."

"Are you sure?" Dan asked doubtfully. "Two hundred dollars doesn't seem like very much."

"Well, they're used," Emily pointed out. "Besides, it isn't really the money that matters to me. I just want them out of the house."

Dan was quiet for a minute. "I see," he said at last. "Well, if you're really sure . . ."

"I am," Emily told him.

"Well, in that case, I have a friend who I think might be really interested in them. His name is Jamie, and he's a sophomore at Palisades. He told me he's been looking a long time for a really good deal. So when I saw your ad . . ."

Emily cleared her throat. "You mean—" *You mean, you're not going to try to talk me out of it?* she was thinking. She couldn't believe her ears. Dan obviously couldn't care less that she was giving up her entire musical career! All he cared about was getting her drums away from her— for some guy over at Palisades!

"As long as you're sure and everything," Dan added hastily. "I mean, I wouldn't want to take them off your hands unless you really mean business, Em. That's why I was trying to find that out first. But if you're sure—"

"I'm sure," Emily said coldly. "You can tell your friend they're all his—as long as he's got the two hundred dollars."

"Great!" Dan exclaimed. "Emily, that's terrific! He's going to be so happy," he added.

Emily didn't respond. She had really thought Dan liked her. The very least he could have done was to pretend to try to make her change her mind!

"Can I come over right away for them?" Dan asked eagerly. "I told Jamie that I'd see if they were available. He's going to call me about them tonight."

"Boy, you sure were prepared," Emily said icily.

"Well," Dan said, surprised, "since they're for sale, I thought I might as well—"

"Fine," Emily cut him off. "Come over whenever you like."

"Emily," Karen called brightly from the hallway. "Are you off the phone yet? I wanted to ask you if you could sit for Karrie tonight."

"Sure," Emily called back, her voice dull. Why not? she thought miserably. It didn't matter that she'd baby-sat for Karrie the previous night. She didn't have anything else to do. That was for sure!

Dan seemed to be in good spirits when he came over. "Now, you haven't had any second thoughts, have you?'' he asked Emily as he followed her downstairs to her studio.

"No," Emily said, trying to keep the emotion out of her voice.

Once they were downstairs Dan didn't seem so cheerful anymore. The studio seemed to make him nervous, as if he were reliving the terrible scene that had taken place Thursday afternoon.

"So," he said awkwardly, not meeting Emily's gaze. "How have you been?"

Emily suddenly felt shy, too. She couldn't help noticing how nice Dan looked. He was wearing jeans, as usual, but he had a maroon polo shirt on that looked really good on him. And she loved his hair. She could see little golden glints in it under the light.

"I've been all right," she said quickly. She wished she could relax around Dan, but every time she looked at him she remembered Karen shouting all those terrible things about her mother.

God knows what he must think of me, she thought. *He's probably told everyone at school about me—about what a liar I am, saying my mother was dead when she really isn't.*

I'll bet he told The Droids, she thought suddenly. *I'll bet they're glad I'm quitting! Maybe this guy Jamie will take my place.*

"I've wanted to talk to you," Dan said softly, staring down at the carpeted floor. "Emily—"

"Why don't we get the drums?" Emily asked

quickly, brushing past him into her studio. She wanted to get this over with—and she wanted Dan to leave. It was just too embarrassing, having him around. She just wanted to close the door on what had happened. She was going to be a completely different person, she told herself, dragging over the drum cases she stored in the basement closet and taking one last, quick look at her drums. Getting rid of her drums was the logical first step to changing.

"What are you doing tonight?" Dan asked her as she helped him load the boxes in the back of his car. "Do you want to go see a movie or something?"

"No, thanks," Emily said, fighting back tears. It felt so horrible to see her drums all packed up in boxes and disappearing into the back of someone's car. And Dan was acting so callous about the whole thing!

"Are you sure?" He looked disappointed.

Emily nodded. "I'm baby-sitting again," she told him. Not that she thought he really cared. He was probably excited to have found his friend a set of drums.

"Well, I guess I'd better give you your money," he said, taking out his wallet. "Two hundred dollars, right?"

Emily swallowed. Once he gave her the money, the drums were really gone. "Yes," she said miserably. "That's what the ad said, isn't it?"

Dan didn't say anything. A minute later he withdrew four crisp fifty-dollar bills and handed them to Emily without a word.

Her first instinct was to push the money away. It almost made her sick to look at it. But she'd started this thing, and now she had to go through with it. "Thanks," she said dully. Walking away without so much as a backward glance, Emily folded the bills in half and shoved them deep inside her pocket. Her heart was pounding like crazy, but she just kept walking toward the house. And she didn't look back.

"Em?" Mr. Mayer tapped softly at Emily's door. When there was no answer, he pushed the door open and stuck his head inside.

"Hi," Emily said sleepily, sitting up on her bed. She couldn't remember falling asleep, but her room had grown dark, so she guessed it was evening already. Her father looked ready to go out. He was wearing a navy-blue blazer and a tie, and she could smell his after-shave as he came over and sat down on the edge of her bed.

"I just wanted to thank you for baby-sitting for us again tonight," he said, putting his hand on her head. "Em, I know things have been kind of rough for you lately. And I want you to know I appreciate the effort you're making."

Emily felt a lump forming in her throat. It was hard enough when her father sided with

Karen or when he got angry. But when he went all soft on her she couldn't stand it; it was too upsetting.

"I'm happy to help out," she said matter-of-factly, swinging her legs over the side of the bed. "Don't give it another thought, Dad."

Her father looked at her closely. "What have you decided to do about The Droids? Is there any way you can convince them to end practice sessions earlier so you can still make curfew?"

Emily stared at the floor. This was not a moment she'd been looking forward to. "I quit The Droids," she told him. "As a matter of fact, I sold my drums today."

Mr. Mayer's eyes darkened. "You . . . Emily, what are you talking about?"

Emily shrugged. "It seemed like too much trouble, that's all. And there wasn't much point in keeping the drums here, anyway. Every time I practiced Karen told me I was waking Karrie."

Mr. Mayer sighed. "You know, I really hoped the three of us could work out a reasonable solution, Em. And the last thing I expected was for you to do anything rash. I appreciate how upset you've been, but I can't see how being a martyr about your music is going to help matters."

Tears spilled down Emily's cheeks. "I am not being a martyr!" she cried. "Dad, you don't know anything about it! I did what I had to," she added. "And to tell you the truth, I'm glad those drums are gone."

"You may feel that way now," Mr. Mayer said grimly, "but what's going to happen when you change your mind? It'll be too late to do anything about it then. Your drums are gone for good now, Emily. What are you going to do if you want them back next week?"

Emily bit her lip. "I won't want them back," she said woodenly. "I never want to play the drums again as long as I live."

"I hope you got some money for them," her father said. "I remember how hard you worked to save up for those drums."

"I got money," Emily said dully, remembering the way she'd felt when Dan had handed her the fifty-dollar bills. "Don't worry, Dad. I know what I'm doing."

"I'll leave the number of where we'll be on the desk in my study," her father told her, getting to his feet.

The minute he'd left the room Emily got off her bed and crossed the room to her desk. After turning on her desk lamp, she opened the bottom drawer in her desk. This had always been the drawer where Emily kept her most private possessions: the first love letter she'd ever received; a blue ribbon from a sixth-grade track meet; and countless certificates of honor for music.

At the back of the drawer Emily had placed an envelope containing the two hundred dollars. She pulled it out and looked inside the envelope at the money. She had no idea what she was going to do with all that money. But just knowing it was there made her feel a little bit better.

Then Emily noticed the corner of an envelope in the clutter of bottom-drawer possessions. She reached into the drawer and pulled a photograph from the envelope.

It was a picture of Emily with her parents at Secca Lake, just outside Sweet Valley. It had been taken the summer before her mother left and was the only really good picture Emily had of her mother. It was hard to make out her father's features in the picture because he was squinting a little in the sun. But her mother . . . her mother looked so beautiful in the picture! Her face was very soft, and she was smiling at some point behind the camera. She looked so gentle, Emily thought. So loving.

But a minute later she had replaced the photograph in her drawer. There was no point in dwelling on the past, she told herself, snapping off the lamp and getting to her feet.

She had to go look in on little Karrie now. Everything else was gone: her mother, her music, Dan. . . . But Emily had promised herself not to weaken. She was going to fit into her father's new life if it killed her. She was going to knock herself out trying to help her stepmother. Because she knew if she didn't, Karen would convince her father that boarding school was the answer. And Emily was afraid that leaving Sweet Valley would really kill her.

Nine

Alice Wakefield took the last load of laundry out of the dryer, shaking the towels out. It was Sunday afternoon, and the house was quiet. Steven had come home for the weekend to see his grandparents, and he and the twins were out at the beach with them.

One week more, Mrs. Wakefield thought, and Grandma and Grandpa Wakefield would go back to Michigan. She wondered if she'd feel any more secure after they were gone. Not that she hadn't enjoyed their visit—she had always been very close to her husband's parents, and this past week she had enjoyed their company even more than usual. It was the twins she was feeling anxious about.

Mrs. Wakefield had tried over and over again to include herself in their plans, but so far she'd struck out every single time. At first she'd tried to tell herself that it didn't matter, that the twins just wanted to be alone with their grandparents. She could hardly blame them for that, could she? They saw their grandparents only once a year, while they saw *her* every single day.

But Mrs. Wakefield couldn't fight the feeling that there was more involved. In the old days, Mrs. Wakefield thought, the twins were always asking her for advice. They wanted to know what she thought of the outfits they wore to school. Or they wanted help with their homework. At the very least they wanted her to help them mend something or show them how to use things in the kitchen.

Now, Mrs. Wakefield thought, they were all grown up. They didn't need her anymore. And they didn't have time for her anymore, either.

But Mrs. Wakefield had a plan. She had already left word at the design firm that she wouldn't be in the next day. It had been ages since she'd taken a day off.

This way, she thought happily, she would be there waiting for the girls when they got home from school. Their grandparents wouldn't be able to steal them away. She could take them shopping—they never seemed to tire of that.

Mrs. Wakefield felt considerably cheered by her plan. In fact, she was so pleased with it that at first she didn't think she'd heard Jessica correctly when she broached the subject to the twins later that afternoon in the living room.

"We can't, Mom," Jessica said. "Grandma's taking us hot-air ballooning."

"What?" Mrs. Wakefield asked.

Jessica was rolling up the sleeves of her T-shirt, an expression of concentration on her pretty face. "You know," she said vaguely. "Hot-air ballooning, Mom. It's going to be great!"

"Grandma has the craziest ideas." Elizabeth giggled. "Can you imagine a woman her age wanting to go flying in one of those things? But she was the one who thought of it. There's a place down at the beach that has the balloons. So Grandma and Grandpa are going to pick us up at school tomorrow, and we're going to take one out before dinner."

"Oh," Mrs. Wakefield said, completely defeated. Hot-air ballooning! How in the world could she hope to compete with that?

"Maybe we could go shopping some other time, Mom," Elizabeth said, looking thoughtfully at her mother. "What do you think, Jess?"

Jessica seemed to be having problems getting her sleeves even. "What?" she asked blankly, staring from Elizabeth to her mother. "Did I miss something?"

"No," Mrs. Wakefield said shortly, getting to her feet. "Don't worry, Jessica. You didn't miss a thing."

"What's wrong with *her*? Did I say something I shouldn't have?" Alice Wakefield could hear Jessica asking indignantly as she left the room.

Well, I give up, Mrs. Wakefield thought, walking into the study. *Obviously I'm not enough fun for them. They don't need me anymore, and I'm just too boring for them.*

"Hey," Mr. Wakefield said, putting the newspaper down. "Why so glum? Is anything wrong?"

Mrs. Wakefield shrugged, then sat down across from him in her favorite chair. "Not unless you consider being useful an important thing." She sighed.

"What are you talking about?"

"It's the girls," Mrs. Wakefield told him. "They just don't need me anymore, Ned. And I guess I'm feeling kind of sad about it."

"How about starting from the beginning?" Mr. Wakefield asked her. "I'm afraid I'm going to need a little bit of filling in on this one."

Alice Wakefield told him exactly how she'd been feeling recently. She told him about her plans to cook a special dinner for everyone and why that hadn't worked. And how she'd been trying hard to get home early so she could spend some time alone with the twins. "That didn't work, either." She sighed again. "Ned, I'm just out of the running, it seems. Your parents are so much fun that I end up seeming like an old stick-in-the-mud." Her voice cracking a little, she told him the latest—about her plan to take a day off from work to take Jessica and Elizabeth shopping. "Guess what your parents suggested?" she asked hollowly.

"What?" Mr. Wakefield asked, smiling sympathetically at his wife. "Big-game hunting? A trip to Disneyland?"

"Worse," Mrs. Wakefield said. "Hot-air ballooning! Ned, how in the world is an ordinary, run-of-the-mill mother supposed to compete with *that*?"

"Alice." Mr. Wakefield grinned. "You are hardly run-of-the-mill. In fact, you're one of the most spectacular women I've ever laid eyes on."

"I may be acting crazy, but I really feel hurt," Mrs. Wakefield said.

"Remember," Mr. Wakefield told her, "their grandparents aren't here very often. They're trying hard to cram everything into a short period of time."

"I know, I know," Mrs. Wakefield said. "I'm being incredibly insecure. But I can't help it! If only the twins would just come to me for one tiny little thing, if they'd just act like they needed me, instead of treating me like a . . . I don't know, a coatrack or something!"

"Honey," Mr. Wakefield said, "just try to hang on a little bit longer. My parents are leaving at the end of the week, and everything'll go back to normal."

"But that's just it!" Mrs. Wakefield cried, anguished. "I don't want things just to go back to normal! I want things to be *better* between the girls and me. Don't you see?"

"Maybe you should talk to them," Mr. Wakefield suggested. "That's been the best route in the past, hasn't it?"

"Yes, but I don't want to pressure them. I don't want to make them feel like they have to—you know, indulge their paranoid mother or something."

"Well, my vote is cast," Mr. Wakefield told her. "I think talking things over is always the best policy."

"All those years in court," Mrs. Wakefield teased him affectionately, "and you still believe things get worked out just by talking?"

"Yep," Mr. Wakefield said, giving her a big smile. "I still do."

Mrs. Wakefield shook her head. In her heart she suspected her husband was right. But she didn't want to have to talk to Elizabeth and Jessica about this. She wanted the girls to come to *her*—to show that they needed her again, all on their own.

Emily took a deep breath and wiped her forehead with the back of her hand as she sat beside the bathtub. She was exhausted. It was hard to believe that taking care of a baby could be so tiring, but it really was. Karrie was getting good at crawling, and the minute Emily put her down she was off like lightning, racing for the first object that caught her eye.

And everything always seemed to happen at

once. Emily would just be in the middle of trying to change little Karrie's diapers, and the phone would ring. Or she'd be playing with Karrie in her bedroom and remember that she'd left something downstairs on the stove. It seemed she needed six hands to get everything done!

"Are you done yet?" Karen asked now, coming into the bathroom.

Emily blinked. "No, I just got her in here," she said.

"I've just about had it." Karen sighed. "As a matter of fact, I was thinking of sneaking over to the mall this afternoon, if you don't mind, Emily. I really need to find a dress for the party the Bronsons are having next weekend."

I guess that means I'm baby-sitting again, Emily thought. *This afternoon and next weekend.*

"You don't mind, do you?" Karen asked, not waiting for Emily to respond. "I'm just getting so claustrophobic, locked up in this house all the time. If your dad gets home, will you tell him where I am?"

Emily nodded, lathering little Karrie's back.

"Maybe you could do something about dinner, too," Karen said absently. "There's some lettuce in the vegetable drawer that you could wash for salad. And I think there's some tomato sauce in the freezer. If you could just—"

"Karen," Emily said, trying to stay calm, "it's kind of hard for me to do two things at once. If

101

I watch Karrie all afternoon, I probably won't be able to get dinner ready, too."

Karen's eyes darkened. "Fine!" she snapped. "Forget I even asked you."

Uh-oh, Emily thought. *I guess I blew it again.*

"For your information," Karen added coldly, taking a tube of lipstick out of the drawer and leaning closer to the mirror to apply it, "I really don't like your tone of voice. I ask very little of you, Emily, and I don't appreciate your attitude."

Wow, Emily thought. *She's in a great mood today!*

Emily was getting tired of her stepmother's ingratitude. She knew how hard Emily had been working around the house. All Emily did anymore was sleep, go to school, and baby-sit!

But Karen didn't care. She still seemed to hate Emily, to be waiting for the least little thing to go wrong so she could snap at her. And Emily had taken just about all she could.

She hoped her father would get home before Karen returned from her shopping trip. She had to talk to her father. She was desperate enough to tell him what Karen had said about her mother. Something was going to have to change—and soon.

"Anyone home?" Mr. Mayer called, setting his golf clubs down inside the storage room off the kitchen. "Karen?"

"Karen isn't here," Emily told him, walking

into the kitchen with Karrie in her arms. "She said to tell you that she's at the mall. She's shopping for something to wear to that party you guys are going to next weekend."

Mr. Mayer leaned over to kiss the nape of Karrie's neck. "My little sweetheart," he crooned, stroking her silky hair.

"She said she'd be back before dinner," Emily added.

"Good," Mr. Mayer said, smiling. "How are you, honey? Did you have a good day?"

"It was so-so," Emily said honestly. There was no time like the present, she told herself. She had to tell him the truth!

"Why just 'so-so'?" her father asked, getting a glass out of the cupboard and opening a bottle of beer.

Emily wrinkled her nose. "I've been baby-sitting a lot lately."

Mr. Mayer took a sip of beer. "That's not so bad, is it? When the baby is a little angel like Karrie?"

Emily bit her lip. She could tell this wasn't going to be easy. "She's great," Emily said unhappily. "But, Dad—"

"Well, what's the problem?" her father asked cheerfully. "Are you having second thoughts about your drums?"

Emily flushed. Sometimes lately she couldn't believe she and her father had once been so close. It struck her that he had almost no idea how she really felt about anything. "No, Dad," she said quietly. "That isn't it. The thing is," she blurted out, "I'm having a hard time with Karen, Dad. I need your help."

Her father set down his glass. For a minute it seemed as if the whole house was hushed. "What kind of problems?" her father asked.

Emily shrugged helplessly. "You know, Daddy! She's always angry with me for something. If I don't do every single little thing she wants me to do, she gets furious with me. I feel like I can't talk to her reasonably," she concluded. "I guess I'm afraid of her. I feel trapped."

"Emily, you know how vulnerable Karen is right now," Mr. Mayer said. "She's going through a very difficult time, adjusting to having a baby around, learning to live with a stepdaughter who's almost fully grown. She's got a lot of pressure on her, and she needs your help."

Emily felt her control beginning to crumble. "What about me, Daddy?" she demanded. "Why doesn't anyone think about what *I* need anymore? Do you think it's been easy for me, having to adjust to a new stepmother and a new baby in the house all at the same time? Don't you care how *I* feel?"

"Emily." Mr. Mayer sighed and picked up his glass of beer. "We've been over this a dozen times. Of course I care how you feel! But I expect a lot from you. I always have. Karen tells me," he added, "that you can be extremely rude to her at times. That bothers me, Em."

"I'm not rude to her," Emily said, her voice quavering. "She's lying, Dad."

Mr. Mayer's eyebrows shot up. "That's quite an accusation," he said evenly. "Are you sure you really mean that?"

Taking a deep breath, Emily began to tell her father what Karen had said about her mother. "She said horrible things, Daddy," Emily told him, tears running down her cheeks. "She called her a tramp . . . in front of my friend Dan . . ."

Mr. Mayer's face was suffused with anger. "I don't want to hear anymore," he said at last, slamming his glass down on the table. Karrie squirmed in Emily's arms and began to cry. "Your stepmother is running this house now," Mr. Mayer raged. "And whatever she says goes. I will *not* tolerate your talking back to her or talking about her behind her back! You are to respect her and to treat her like a member of the family. Do you hear me?"

"Yes," Emily whispered, the color draining from her face.

The next minute her father stormed out of the kitchen.

"Don't cry," Emily crooned, stroking Karrie's head gently with her free hand. "Don't cry, Karrie. Everything's going to be all right."

But Emily's voice was quavering. And when she bent over to kiss the baby's forehead, her own face was wet with tears.

Ten

"That was fabulous!" Jessica exclaimed. "Grandma, can we go hot-air ballooning again before you go? I could do that again and again!"

"Not me." Elizabeth groaned and clutched at her stomach. "Grandma, I don't know how you do it," she added, putting her arm around her grandmother. "I thought I was going to faint when we started bumping around up there."

"That was the best part," Jessica protested. "Everything looked so incredibly tiny from high up! It was perfect," she added. "Absolutely perfect."

"Just between you and me," Elizabeth whispered to her twin, "I think I could live a long time without doing that again."

Jessica shook her head. "I hate to change the subject," she said, "but what's going on with Emily? I haven't seen her around at lunch lately."

Elizabeth's brow furrowed. "I haven't either. I called her last night, but her father said she'd gone to bed early. I'm really worried about her."

"Does Dan have her drums in a safe place?"

Elizabeth nodded. "Still, that isn't going to help if she doesn't care enough to look for them. There must be something we can do to help, but I just can't think of what to do."

The twins followed their grandparents into the kitchen. They were so engrossed in their conversation that they barely noticed the expression on their mother's face as they entered.

"How was it up there?" Mrs. Wakefield asked brightly, trying to look cheerful. "Does anyone need a snack after all that exertion?"

"We had a wonderful time, Mom!" Jessica answered, her eyes shining. "Didn't we, Liz?"

Elizabeth laughed. "It was fun. A little hard on the stomach, but fun."

"I was thinking," Mrs. Wakefield said tentatively, "that we might all go out for Mexican food tonight. Does that sound good?"

"I don't know, Mom," Elizabeth said. "I'm not sure my stomach is really ready for burritos right now."

"I know what," Grandma Wakefield said briskly. "Bob and I will whip something up right here in the kitchen. Maybe just some soup and sandwiches or something."

"I'll help," Jessica volunteered.

"And I'll set the table," Elizabeth seconded

quickly. Neither of them noticed that their mother had left the kitchen.

"Hey," Mr. Wakefield said about an hour later, coming into the kitchen and setting his briefcase down, "do you think I can steal away these identical elves of yours for just a few minutes?"

"Sure." Grandpa Wakefield laughed, as he stirred the soup that was simmering on the stove. "They've done too much to help us as it is."

"What's up, Dad?" Elizabeth asked as she and Jessica followed him into the study.

"Uh-oh," Jessica said, watching her father close the door behind him. "It looks serious, Liz. What've we done this time?"

Mr. Wakefield laughed. "Come on," he protested. "I just want to talk with you two, that's all."

"We're listening, Dad," Elizabeth assured him. "What's going on?"

"Actually, something *is* wrong," Mr. Wakefield admitted. "It's your mother. Have either of you noticed anything strange about the way she's been acting lately?"

"Sort of," Elizabeth said, catching Jessica's eye. "Why?" she asked. "She's OK, isn't she?"

Jessica took a cue from her sister's anxiety and began to panic. "Is she sick?" she asked, jumping out of her chair. "Dad, what's wrong with her? You have to tell us!"

Mr. Wakefield burst out laughing. "Nothing's wrong with her," he assured them. "Nothing physical, anyway," he added, settling back in his chair. "Girls, I think your mother is suffering from a very common complaint, but one that's almost never given proper attention."

"What is it, Dad?" Elizabeth managed weakly.

"She feels left out," Mr. Wakefield announced. He waited for a minute for his words to sink in before continuing. "She feels as though her kids are so grown up they don't need her anymore. And it seems to her that they have better things to do with their spare time than hang around with their mother."

"Oh, no," Elizabeth groaned. "Jess, we've been so thoughtless lately! Remember how crushed Mom looked when Grandma and Grandpa took us out for Chinese food and she'd been planning that big dinner?"

"But that was Dad's fault," Jessica pointed out. "Sorry, Dad," she amended quickly, "but you're the one who doesn't like Chinese food."

"And what about this afternoon?" Elizabeth continued. "You saw how excited she was about taking us shopping, Jess! And instead we went off in that terrible hot-air balloon with Grandma and Grandpa."

"It wasn't terrible," Jessica protested. "It was excellent, Liz!"

"OK, OK." Mr. Wakefield sighed. "There's no point in blaming yourselves. The truth is, you two have been eager to spend as much time as possible with your grandparents, which is perfectly natural. And your mother understands that. But she's only human. She can't help feeling a little bit lonesome when you're all off together having a wonderful time. What I was wondering," he concluded, folding his arms across his chest the way he always did when he was deep in thought, "is what we can all do to get her out of the doldrums before Grandma and Grandpa leave. Any ideas?"

"Do you think Mom would like hot-air ballooning?" Jessica asked.

Elizabeth groaned. "Jessica, we can do a lot better than that," she said.

"I don't doubt it," Mr. Wakefield declared. "I can't think of a twosome better at scheming than my own daughters. And I knew if I alerted you, you'd be able to take care of it."

Jessica and Elizabeth exchanged glances. Elizabeth wondered if perhaps their father was overconfident. From the way it sounded, this was kind of a large order to fill. How could they make it clear to their mother that they needed her more than ever, without making it obvious what they were doing?

"Hey," Jessica said, "I have an idea! Come on, Liz," she cried, grabbing Elizabeth by the arm and pulling her out of the study.

"Thanks, Dad," Elizabeth called behind her. She was glad Jessica was taking charge. Elizabeth was genuinely worried about their mother, and the sooner they could put things right again, the better she would feel.

Mrs. Wakefield was upstairs, riffling through a stack of photographs when the twins found her.

"Mom," Jessica said solemnly, almost knocking Elizabeth over in her haste to get into the bedroom first, "we have an important question to ask you. Don't we, Liz?"

Elizabeth nodded. "Are you busy?" she asked. "We could come back later."

"No," Mrs. Wakefield said quickly. "I was just looking at some old pictures. What's up?"

"Well, we were thinking . . ." Elizabeth began, looking at her twin out of the corner of her eye. "It's been so wonderful having Grandma and Grandpa here. We were thinking it would be really nice to do something special for them before they go."

"After all," Jessica chimed in, "they've done so much for us!"

"I know," Mrs. Wakefield said, organizing the photographs in her hand. "You're very lucky," she added flatly. "You have terrific grandparents."

"Don't you think it would be nice to have a

special dinner for them before they go?" Jessica asked.

"Not just a dinner," Elizabeth mused. "A kind of going-away party."

"That would be very nice," Mrs. Wakefield said, trying to look enthusiastic. "I'm sure Grandma and Grandpa would love it."

What about you? Elizabeth was thinking. Suddenly she ached all over with sympathy for her mother. She was so selfless, so willing to give her and Jessica anything they wanted. And when she'd needed attention, they'd just ignored her.

"The thing is," she said quietly, looking straight into her mother's eyes, "we don't want Grandma and Grandpa to know about the party. And to be honest, we could really use some help."

"That's right," Jessica seconded. "I mean, we have no idea what to do. Do you think it should be a sit-down dinner? Or should we have a buffet the way you did the last time you had a party? And what about—"

"Wait!" Mrs. Wakefield laughed, putting her hands up. "One thing at a time," she added. "First of all, do you want to have guests, or just family?"

Elizabeth and Jessica stared at each other. "We hadn't really thought about that," Elizabeth admitted.

"Well, that's a good place to start," Mrs. Wakefield said wryly. "And what sort of food do you want to have? We can't decide about buffet versus sit-down before you've decided that."

"Well, we really weren't sure," Jessica admitted. "On the one hand, we'd like it to be something really special. But we don't want to spend a million dollars, either."

Mrs. Wakefield shook her head. "I should hope not," she said. "Well, the thing to do," she added, "is to make a list. Start with your guests and then figure out what kind of food will be most appropriate. And," she said suddenly, "what about decorations? Jessica, you did such a nice job the night that Grandma and Grandpa arrived. Do you think you'd want something like that again?"

Elizabeth caught her sister's eye. *It's working,* she thought happily. Their mother sounded like her old self again—involved, enthusiastic, having a good time.

Elizabeth was so glad now that their father had alerted them. And Jessica's idea was absolutely perfect—especially, Elizabeth thought, because it was legitimate. They really did want to have a party for their grandparents. And they really did need their mother's help. If only they could convey that to her, maybe she wouldn't feel so left out anymore. Then she could relax and enjoy the rest of the visit with Grandma and Grandpa Wakefield.

* * *

Emily was downstairs in the family room, trying to work on a current-events report for history and keep an eye on little Karrie at the same time. It was Thursday evening, and she was already behind on her homework for the week.

And Karen had just told her she needed her to baby-sit again. "I'm going over to visit with my parents," Karen announced, standing in the doorway and frowning at Emily. "I'll be home around ten. Your father has to do a lot of paperwork tonight, so can you just watch Karrie for me until I'm back?"

Emily nodded.

"All she needs is a bath," Karen added, looking quickly at her watch. "If anything comes up, my parents' number is on the desk."

Emily nodded again but didn't say anything.

Karen knelt down next to the baby, who was sitting on a large blanket on the floor, and handed her a brand-new toy, a little rag doll with braided hair and two beads that were supposed to be eyes.

"Look what Mommy brought you," Karen crooned sweetly. "A little dolly for you to play with!"

"Hey," Emily said suddenly, taking the doll out of Karrie's hands, "I don't think those beads are on tight enough, Karen. The one on the left looks—"

"Emily, for God's sake," Karen said sharply, grabbing the toy away from her.

Emily took a deep breath. It wasn't fair, she was thinking. She spent so much time with Karrie that she couldn't help feeling protective of her!

Karen handed the doll right back to Karrie. "Don't worry, sweetie," she crooned. "Mommy won't let Emily take away your little doll."

Just then the telephone rang, and Karen scooped up Karrie, then picked up the family-room extension. Emily sighed and returned to her notebook. It looked like another long evening was ahead of her, she thought.

Karen set Karrie down beside her on the couch. The baby still had the doll in her hand. Apparently it was Karen's mother on the phone. They were arguing about the photo album Karen had promised to bring over. "But, Mother—" Karen said sharply, toying with the telephone cord. "No, Mother—"

Boy, I'd hate to have to spend an evening with those two, Emily thought, not looking up from her homework. Karen was so intent on her conversation that she didn't realize that Karrie had just succeeded in pulling the loose bead off her doll. Making a little cooing noise, the baby studied the button from all angles.

"Mother, I told you—" Karen said angrily.

Karrie popped the bead in her mouth.

The next thing Emily knew, all hell had bro-

116

ken loose. Karen dropped the telephone, scream-
ing. Little Karrie had swallowed the bead, and
it was obvious that she was choking. Her
tiny face had turned a faint bluish color, and
tears were spilling from her eyes. But she
couldn't make a noise. The bead was blocking
her tiny windpipe, and she wasn't getting any
air.

"Karrie! Karrie!" her mother screamed, grabbing the baby and shaking her. Emily could
hear Karen's mother's voice, alarmed and high-
pitched, calling something from the receiver dangling from the coffee table.

"She's choking!" Emily hollered, jumping to
her feet.

It was apparent to Emily that Karen had no
idea what to do. And unless someone did something right away, Karrie was going to choke to
death, right before their eyes.

"Give her to me!" Emily said, grabbing Karen
by the shoulders and turning her around.

But by this point Karen was hysterical. And
she was hanging onto her baby with all her
strength.

Unless Emily could get Karrie out of her arms,
the baby was going to suffocate. Emily didn't
even stop to think. She had read somewhere
that the best thing to do when someone was
hysterical was to slap him or her. And that was
exactly what Emily did.

She slapped her stepmother as hard as she could, right across her face. Then she took advantage of Karen's momentary shock to snatch Karrie out of her arms.

Eleven

Emily knew exactly what to do. She had taken a first-aid class at the civic center the previous year, and she had learned how to deliver the Heimlich maneuver to save choking victims. Emily had been taught to give the maneuver to older children and adults, but she assumed it would work on a baby as well.

Holding the baby firmly on her lap, Emily put both her hands together just about little Karrie's stomach. Forming a double fist with her hands, she jerked back sharply, putting sudden pressure on Karrie's diaphragm. The bead popped out of Karrie's mouth, and the baby started to scream.

Emily's eyes filled with tears. She'd saved the baby's life. Karrie could breathe again.

"Give her to me!" Karen yelled, rushing over and grabbing Karrie out of Emily's arms.

"What's going on here?" Mr. Mayer demanded, storming into the room.

The scene that greeted him was alarming. The phone receiver, still dangling from the coffee table, was bleating now. A chair had been turned over, and everyone in the room was crying—Karen, Emily, and Karrie, whose face was rapidly assuming its natural color as each cry pumped fresh air into her lungs.

"Answer me!" Mr. Mayer yelled, his own face turning bright red.

But it didn't look as if anyone could speak yet. Emily felt faint. She grabbed the desk to steady herself, looking helplessly at her stepmother. *Tell him*, she was thinking desperately. *Tell Daddy what happened.*

But Karen seemed to be in a state of shock. All she could do was shake her head, weeping, and hug little Karrie more tightly.

"What have you done now?" Mr. Mayer shouted, turning to Emily.

"I haven't done anything!" Emily cried hoarsely, still hanging onto the desk. "Honestly, Daddy. I was just—"

"I've heard enough," her father said grimly. "I've heard the same thing over and over again, and I'm sick and tired of it. Leave the room!" he shouted. "Go upstairs and stay upstairs until I tell you you can come down!"

Emily burst into tears. "Daddy, I didn't do anything wrong! Karen, tell him," she begged, turning imploringly to her stepmother. "Tell him I was just trying to help."

Karen was still crying. "Karrie," she moaned brokenly. "My poor little angel—my poor little baby—"

Mr. Mayer's face went white. "Did you try to hurt little Karrie?" he demanded, turning back to Emily with a look on his face that she'd never seen before.

"No," she whispered hoarsely, staring at him.

"Get out," her father said savagely, crossing the room in two strides to encircle Karen and the baby with his arms. "You heard me," he added, glaring at her from across the room. *"Just get out."*

Well, she was getting out, all right, Emily thought, running upstairs. Racing across her room, Emily jerked open the bottom drawer of her desk. "Where is it?" she cried, tears blinding her eyes. At last her fumbling fingers brushed the envelope at the back of the drawer. The money was still there. She put it in her shoulder bag.

She was halfway across her room when something occurred to her. Crossing back to her desk, Emily opened the drawer again. Taking out the photograph of her mother, she slipped it into her bag.

"Goodbye, room," she said aloud, taking one last look around her. And then she ran down the stairs and out the front door, slamming it as hard as she could behind her.

An hour later Emily was sitting in the Box Tree Café, a popular Sweet Valley restaurant. An empty plate and a glass with melted ice in it were sitting in front of her. Emily could barely remember finishing her soda or eating the dessert she'd ordered. As a matter of fact, she couldn't really remember coming into the restaurant. Everything that had happened since she had run out of the house was a blur.

Emily wasn't used to being in a restaurant by herself, especially not at night. It was almost seven-thirty now, and the tables around her were filled with families enjoying their dinners and chattering and laughing. But Emily barely noticed them. She had to have a plan, she thought, taking her address book out of her purse. She had to figure out what she was going to do.

Her first thought was to call Elizabeth Wakefield. The Wakefields wouldn't let her stay at their house for more than a day or two—not without notifying her father. But at least they'd put her up for the night. And by this time the next day she'd be far away.

Too far for anyone to find her.

From the minute she took her mother's photograph out of her desk drawer, Emily knew what she would have to do. *I'm going to find her,* she told herself grimly, pushing the remaining pieces of ice in her glass around with the straw. *I'll get out to Chicago somehow and find her.*

Emily's eyes filled with tears. She hadn't heard a word from her mother since she was ten years old. At first, right after her mother left, there were some letters. Those were less frequent after a while, and Emily heard from her mother only on birthdays and Christmas. Then, just on her birthdays. And then . . .

I don't care, she thought stubbornly, getting up and walking over to the pay phone. *She's all I've got left now. It's obvious my father doesn't want me. My mother's the only hope I have left.*

But when Emily put her change into the pay phone, she didn't call directory assistance in Chicago, as she'd planned. Instead, she dialed the Wakefields' number.

"Emily!" Elizabeth cried. "I've been trying to get in touch with you for ages. How are you?"

"Not good," Emily said softly, keeping her voice down so no one in the restaurant could hear her. "As a matter of fact, I'm . . ." Her voice trailed off uncertainly.

"Where are you?" Elizabeth demanded, alarmed.

"I'm at the Box Tree Café," Emily said. "Liz, do you think I could come over? I really need to talk to you."

"Of course you can," Elizabeth said. "Why don't you stay right there, and I'll come pick you up."

"OK," Emily said weakly. She didn't feel like walking all the way over to the Wakefields' house. Suddenly she was tired. Really tired. Right then what she wanted more than anything in the world was to crawl into bed and sleep.

Maybe the next day she would feel stronger, she told herself. Strong enough to find her mother's number, call her up, and ask her if she could go out to Chicago and live with her.

Feeling dazed, Emily replaced the receiver and went back to her table to get the bill. She was numb. It seemed that all she could do was to collapse into her chair and wait for Elizabeth to come get her and take her home.

Elizabeth had already warned the entire family that Emily was in some kind of trouble. "It sounds serious," she concluded, grabbing her car keys and slipping on her nylon jacket. "I'm going to run over to the Box Tree and pick her up, OK?"

"Do me a favor, Liz," Mrs. Wakefield said. "After you've picked Emily up, would you mind stopping at the supermarket? We're out of milk."

"Sure, Mom," Elizabeth said, hurrying out to the front hall. *Poor Emily*, she was thinking. *I hope everything's all right.*

She thought about Emily's situation as she drove across town, checking for traffic every now and then in the rearview mirror of the Fiat Spider that she and Jessica shared.

Elizabeth had become very fond of Emily since the girl had taken her into her confidence. But at the same time she still felt uneasy about offering Emily advice. She wanted so much to help her, but she wasn't sure what approach was best.

If Elizabeth had been nervous about what to say to Emily when she picked her up, she needn't have worried. Emily did all the talking. She had been in the car only for a minute or two when she began to tell Elizabeth everything that had happened since the Thursday night when the twins and their grandparents had dropped her off back home.

Only one thread of the story she told Elizabeth was familiar—the part about Dan buying her drums for his friend Jamie.

The rest of the story shocked Elizabeth deeply. She found it almost impossible to imagine the scene that had taken place at the Mayers' house that night. How could Karen have just stood by in silence while Mr. Mayer accused Emily of hurting little Karrie after Emily had saved the baby's life?

"That's awful," Elizabeth said at last, shaking her head as she pulled into the parking lot in front of the local supermarket. "Emily, what are you going to do?"

"I'm going to Chicago," Emily said in a low voice. "I'm going to find out my mother's number, and I'm going to call her and ask her if I can move in with her."

Elizabeth was shocked. "Can you do that?" she asked. "Can you just pick up and move halfway across the country, Emily?"

"I have the money Dan gave me for my drums," Emily said stubbornly. "I'm sure I can afford bus fare to Chicago. And my mother can take care of me once I get there."

Elizabeth shook her head. "Wow," she said at last. "What about talking to your father? I know he acted horribly tonight, but maybe if you explained everything to him again, maybe he'd—"

"I don't think so," Emily said firmly. "I tried that, Liz. And it didn't work. There's no point in telling him where I'm going, either. He'd never understand."

Elizabeth bit her lip. "Stay right here," she urged Emily. "I've just got to run inside for a second and pick up a carton of milk. Do you need anything?"

Emily shook her head.

Pocketing her keys, Elizabeth hurried inside the brightly lit supermarket. Her mind was buzzing with everything Emily had just told her. Was Emily serious about leaving town? It sure seemed like it! But how could she just take off without even telling her father where she was going?

Suddenly Elizabeth realized that Emily wasn't

the only one with a conflict. She herself had a conflict, she thought, absently choosing a carton of milk from the refrigerated section. Could she just let Emily take off without calling her father and letting him know what she was about to do?

Everything had seemed so simple before Emily started talking about running away. Now Elizabeth had no idea what to do.

Elizabeth was so absorbed that she barely noticed that the blond boy at the check-out counter was smiling at her. "Liz," he said finally, laughing. "Don't you say hello to your friends these days?"

"Eddie!" Elizabeth exclaimed. "How long have you been working here?"

Eddie Strong was a sophomore at Sweet Valley High, and Elizabeth had gotten to know him at *The Oracle*. He was interested in graphics, and he had done some layouts for Mr. Collins.

"Just for a month," Eddie told her. "I'm trying to get some extra money so I can take a trip somewhere this summer."

Elizabeth smiled pleasantly at him, trying not to show how upset and anxious she was. Ordinarily she would have been happy to chat with a friend from school. But she knew how tired Emily was, and she thought it was unfair to leave her alone much longer.

"Hey, have you seen Regina since she got

back?" Eddie asked, taking the bills she gave him and handing her some change.

"Regina?" Elizabeth's eyes widened. "You mean Regina Morrow?"

Eddie laughed. "You don't know any other Reginas, do you?"

Elizabeth was dumbfounded. "But what's she doing back in town? She's supposed to be in the middle of her treatments in Switzerland!"

Eddie shrugged. "Don't ask me. I'm a delivery boy as well as a check-out clerk. Last night I made a delivery to the Morrows' house. That's when I saw Regina. She and her aunt had just come in from the airport."

Elizabeth pocketed her change. "Thanks, Eddie," she said, walking slowly toward the door marked Exit.

Regina Morrow back in town—with her aunt? Elizabeth couldn't believe Regina hadn't written her about it. They had been keeping in touch, and the last Elizabeth had heard, Regina wasn't planning to come back to Sweet Valley at any time in the near future.

Besides, Bruce Patman hadn't mentioned it. And Bruce was hardly the type not to broadcast the fact that his girlfriend was about to drop in from Switzerland for a visit!

Regina Morrow had just enrolled at Sweet Valley High that year. Regina appeared to be the sort of girl who had everything. The daughter of the wealthy owner of a big computer company, she was absolutely beautiful, with raven-black, shiny hair and gorgeous blue eyes. And she was sweet. From the minute her family moved into the enormous estate on the hill overlooking Sweet Valley, everyone had liked Regina.

There was only one thing about Regina that wasn't perfect. She was almost entirely deaf.

Elizabeth had befriended Regina soon after she moved to Sweet Valley. She liked Regina a lot and felt protective toward her new friend. For that reason she had been less than overjoyed when Regina started dating Bruce Patman, the only son of one of the oldest and richest families in Sweet Valley. Bruce was a senior, a tall, handsome boy with dark hair and an engaging smile. The license plates on his black Porsche gave away his image of himself—1 BRUCE 1. Elizabeth had feared that Bruce would hurt Regina, but in fact he had changed a great deal, due to her influence.

For several months Regina had been undergoing treatments in Bern, Switzerland, where a world-famous ear specialist thought he might be able to restore her hearing. Since Regina had been there, Elizabeth had exchanged letters with her on a regular basis. Now she was puzzled about what Eddie had just told her. Still, the Morrows were wealthy enough to make spontaneous decisions, she reminded herself. Maybe Regina was feeling homesick and had persuaded her parents to let her come back to Sweet Valley for a visit.

In any case, Elizabeth made a mental note to drive over to the Morrow estate in the next couple of days to say hello. Regina would probably be busy, but at least Elizabeth could welcome her back!

For now, though, Elizabeth had to keep her attention on Emily. This time she wasn't going to have to invent an occasion to need her mother's advice, she thought ruefully, hurrying across the parking lot to the little red Fiat. This time she really did need to know what Mrs. Wakefield thought.

Elizabeth had no idea what to do about Emily and Mr. Mayer. But from the way Emily was talking about bus tickets, Elizabeth sensed that there was no time to lose!

Twelve

By the time Elizabeth and Emily got back home, it was almost nine o'clock.

"Hi," Elizabeth called, opening the front door. "We're back!"

Instantly Elizabeth and Emily were surrounded. Everyone wanted to know if Emily was all right, if she felt like talking, or if she'd rather be by herself.

"Would you mind if I went upstairs?" Emily asked. "I'm really exhausted. If I could just lie down. . . ."

Mrs. Wakefield put her arm around the brunette. "Come on upstairs with me," she said. "Girls, I think we'll have Emily lie down in Liz's room. That seems easiest for now."

For now, Elizabeth thought. *What are we going to do about Mr. Mayer, though?* She was sure her father wasn't going to let Emily stay even for just one night without letting Mr. Mayer know where she was. But she knew Emily wasn't going to like that idea at all.

Elizabeth decided she'd have to go upstairs and talk to Emily before she fell asleep.

Emily was sitting at the worktable sorting through the contents of her purse, when Elizabeth went in. "I'm trying to find the last phone number my mother gave me," she explained, digging out her address book. "I don't know if it'll help the operator, but it's better than nothing."

"You didn't want to tell my parents about trying to find your mother, did you?" Elizabeth asked.

Emily shook her head. "Your parents wouldn't understand," she said in a low voice. "They're such wonderful people. They would never believe it if I told them what happened tonight."

Elizabeth sat down on the edge of her bed. "Em, I've got to talk to you," she began slowly. "I don't know what my parents are going to say about trying to find your mother or running off to Chicago. I really don't. But I do know"—she took a deep breath—"they won't like the thought of your staying here tonight if your father doesn't know where you are. They're going to want to call him, Emily."

Emily jumped to her feet, her eyes flashing. "They can't!" she burst out. "Please," she said. "I just can't go through another scene like the one tonight. Can you understand that?"

Elizabeth nodded. The awful thing was, she *could* understand. But she wasn't certain she'd be able to convince her parents.

"I'll tell you what," she said at last, getting slowly to her feet. "I'll go downstairs and talk to my mother and find out what she thinks. Maybe I can persuade my parents to leave everything, just for tonight. And tomorrow—"

"Tomorrow," Emily said fiercely, "I'll be on the bus for Chicago. And nothing anybody can say or do is going to stop me!"

"Mom," Elizabeth said, going into the kitchen where her mother and Jessica were discussing recipes for the dinner party they were planning for Saturday night, "I need to talk to you. It's about Emily," she added, sitting down at the kitchen table.

"How is she?" Mrs. Wakefield asked.

"Not good." Elizabeth sighed. "She had a pretty terrible argument with her father and her stepmother this evening. She's decided she can't stay at home anymore."

"Oh, no," Mrs. Wakefield said. "Liz, tell me what happened."

Drawing in a deep breath, Elizabeth told her everything she knew about the events that had taken place at the Mayers' that evening. When she got to the part where little Karrie's life was in danger, Jessica's face went pale.

"God, how horrible for poor Emily," she commiserated. "Is the baby OK?"

"That's the ironic thing," Elizabeth told her. "Emily saved the baby's life. She learned how to treat choking victims in a first-aid class she took last year."

"Oh, thank heavens," Mrs. Wakefield said. "But what went wrong?" she asked, perplexed. "I'd have thought her stepmother would've forgiven her anything after Emily saved her little girl!"

"So would I," Elizabeth agreed. "That's the bizarre part of the story. Apparently everyone was so confused they hardly knew which end was up. But when Mr. Mayer came into the room, he thought everything was Emily's fault. And he blew up at her."

"That's terrible!" Jessica cried. "Didn't Karen stick up for her?"

Elizabeth sighed. "I guess not. She didn't say much of anything, according to Emily. She was just crying and hanging on to Karrie for dear life."

"Well, she was probably shaken up," Mrs. Wakefield pointed out. "After all, she'd just watched her baby practically choke to death. Maybe she explained everything after Emily left the house."

"Well, I suggested as much to Emily," Elizabeth told her mother. "The thing is, Emily's not feeling very forgiving about the whole incident. She's determined not to go back home."

134

"What's she planning to do?" Jessica asked.

Elizabeth took a deep breath. "Well, she wants to try to get in touch with her mother somehow."

"You mean she's leaving Sweet Valley?" Jessica said, aghast.

Elizabeth nodded. "She's convinced that her father will send her off to boarding school if she stays here, anyway. And Emily couldn't stand that. She wants a real family—people to live with who care about her."

"But her mother . . ." Mrs. Wakefield looked thoughtful. "I wish I could imagine a happy outcome to this story, but it strikes me that a mother who's been out of touch for so long might not be overjoyed to find her full-grown daughter on her doorstep, out of the blue."

"I know." Elizabeth sighed. "That's the terrible thing. I think Emily's refusing even to consider what'll happen if her mother won't take her in. The way she's talking, her mother's the only hope she has left. If she can't find her or if her mother won't agree to let her come stay with her . . ." Elizabeth shuddered. "I don't know what will happen then."

Mrs. Wakefield was deep in thought. "The first thing to decide is what to do right now," she said. "Emily can't do anything tonight. But if she stays here," she added, her face clouding over, "your father is going to insist that she call home first to let them know she's safe."

"Emily won't even consider talking to them,"

135

Elizabeth said in a low voice. "I thought of that already, Mom, so I sounded her out on the idea. And she said no way."

Mrs. Wakefield shook her head. "I'm afraid we really can't consider anything else, Liz. Can you imagine how your father and I would feel if either you or Jess were in some kind of trouble? We'd be out of our minds with worry!"

"It doesn't sound like Mr. Mayer and Karen care very much about Emily, though," Jessica argued. "Not after the way they acted tonight!"

"Still," Mrs. Wakefield said, "it's almost impossible to tell from the outside what really goes on in a family. Remember, we're only hearing Emily's side."

"Mom," Elizabeth said slowly, "Emily won't call her father, whatever we say to her. Do you think it would be really unethical for one of us to call the Mayers? At least that way they'd know she was safe."

"Sounds like tattling to me," Jessica commented. "If I were Emily, Liz, I'd never speak to you again if you did something like that!"

"Actually, Jess, Liz has a point," Mrs. Wakefield mused. "If Emily really is dead set against calling home, it may be our only option."

Elizabeth's face colored as she looked across the table at her twin. "I don't want to hurt Emily," she said. "I want to do what's right."

"Of course you do, honey," Mrs. Wakefield said, squeezing her hand. "Liz, I think that's the best we can possibly do for her right now. And I think you should be the one to call Mr. Mayer," she added, getting up from the table.

"Me?" Elizabeth cried, shocked. "Mom, I can't call him! I was thinking that you—"

"Just tell him that Emily is safe and that she's staying over here tonight. Don't worry, honey." Her mother laughed and tousled Elizabeth's hair. "You're one of the most diplomatic people I know. It'll be all right."

"Rat!" Jessica hissed, bouncing out of her chair and leaving the room.

Elizabeth took a deep breath. She couldn't stand the thought of doing something like this behind Emily's back. And Jessica's name-calling was hardly making her feel better about it.

But she couldn't see that she had much choice. *Here goes nothing*, Elizabeth thought. Picking up the receiver in the kitchen, she began to dial the Mayers' number.

Emily was sitting on the bed in Elizabeth's room, her head in her hands. She was trying as hard as she could not to cry, but after the conversation she'd just had, it was all she could do not to break down.

Right after Elizabeth had left the room, Emily dialed the number of the apartment where her mother had been living the last time they'd been in touch. That was almost four years earlier, and she really hadn't expected her mother would still be there. She had charged the call to her father's number so the Wakefields wouldn't get stuck with the bill, and after almost ten rings a woman answered the phone. But it wasn't her mother.

Emily explained who she was, and the woman exclaimed, "You mean Joanne Edwards is your mother!"

"That's right," Emily said. Edwards was her mother's maiden name, and she had been using it since the divorce became final.

"Of course I remember her. She and I used to share this apartment. But her name isn't Edwards any more. She got married."

Married! Emily's heart started to pound. Her mother had gotten married again and had never let her know? She couldn't believe it.

"Where . . . do you know where she went after she got married?" she asked, her mouth dry.

"I'm not sure," the woman said. "She moved out about two years ago. But I think she may have gone to Mexico. Supposedly this guy she married was Mexican. Didn't she write you and let you know?"

"No," Emily said, staring at the wall. "No, she didn't."

She barely heard anything else the woman told her. *She never even wrote*, Emily thought. *She left the country with some man and never even let me know she was going.*

Emily could never remember feeling so alone in her whole life. She couldn't even begin to think about what she was going to do now. She could hardly go chasing around Mexico after a woman who didn't care enough about her to even send a postcard mentioning that she had gotten married again!

Emily was so numb she didn't even notice the door opening.

"Excuse me," a gentle voice broke in. "Can I come in? I was just passing your room, and I saw the light."

Tears stinging in her eyes, Emily looked up at Grandma Wakefield's creased, loving face. "You're welcome to come in," she said brokenly. "It isn't *my* room," she added sharply.

Grandma Wakefield sat down on the edge of Elizabeth's bed, looking searchingly at Emily before she spoke. "You know, I study history," she said at last. "Maybe I like it more as I get older because I have a greater respect for things that happened a long time ago. Who knows? But I was wondering," she said shyly, "if you'd mind listening to a piece of my personal history. It's something I haven't told the twins," she added.

"Go ahead," Emily said miserably. It hardly mattered now, she was thinking.

"Well," Grandma Wakefield said, shifting slightly on the bed to make herself more comfortable, "here goes. The story is really about how I first came to live with Bob, my husband. Or maybe it's more about . . . well, when I met Bob I fell in love with him right away. He was so wonderful." Her face softened as she remembered. "Bob had been married before, but I didn't know that right away. His first wife was killed in a terrible train accident. And she left the most beautiful little boy, whose name was Louis.

"Well, by the time I met Bob, Louis was eleven years old. And he didn't really like the thought of his father getting married to anyone else. His mother was a wonderful woman, and he didn't want anyone to try to replace her."

Emily sat up straighter, listening more closely.

"To make a long story short, Bob and I got married, and a year later, I gave birth to my own little boy, Edward. Only he goes by Ned now, and you know him as Mr. Wakefield. Well, you can't imagine how I felt when that baby was born. I went haywire! Everything had to be just perfect for him. I think I sort of went off the deep end for the first few months. And Louis . . ." Her face clouded over. "Well, Louis was just becoming a teenager. He had his own life, his own set of problems. The last thing he needed was a new mother—or a new baby in the house. It was a rough time for us all."

"But you were never cruel to Louis, were you?" Emily demanded. "I can't imagine you being unfair to anyone!"

Grandma Wakefield smiled. "You're very generous, Emily. But I wouldn't be a very good historian if I weren't objective. And the truth is, I *was* unfair to Louis. I was brand new at being a wife, and brand new at being a mother, too. I had a teenage boy to take care of! I didn't know how to deal with him. I'm afraid I was pretty clumsy for quite a while. I loved him," she concluded, staring down at the carpet. "Oh, yes, I loved him. But there was so much awkwardness between us! I was more than a little afraid of him. And I made all sorts of mistakes."

"Whatever happened to him?" Emily demanded.

"Well, Louis and I got better with each other, bit by bit. But it didn't happen overnight, Emily. In fact, it took years. By the time he was old enough to go to college, I'd almost forgotten he wasn't my own son. And as the years went by, I completely forgot those early years. As far as I'm concerned, Louis and Ned are both my sons now. But when I heard your story the other night, Emily, the historian in me suddenly remembered everything that had been buried for so long."

"Oh, Grandma Wakefield!" Emily cried, throwing her arms around the plump, kindly woman. "I wish I had a grandmother like you," she sobbed, lifting her tear-streaked face to stare up into Grandma Wakefield's eyes.

"Oh, child." Grandma Wakefield clutched Emily tightly to her. "Everything's going to be all right," she told her, stroking her hair and rocking her as if she were a baby. "Everything's going to be just fine."

Emily felt something break inside her as Grandma Wakefield's voice continued its soothing refrain. It was as though a dam had burst, and the tears just poured out of her. She cried as if she would never stop.

She was crying so hard, in fact, that she was oblivious to anything besides her own pounding heart and Grandma Wakefield's soothing hand stroking her hair. She didn't hear the car turn in the driveway below or see the bright ovals of light as headlights flashed across the walls of Elizabeth's room.

In fact, it wasn't until the door bell rang that Emily came out of her reverie. Jumping up, she flew to the window, then turned to face the twins' grandmother. "It's Daddy," she whispered, staring down at the driveway. "Daddy and Karen . . . and Karrie."

Neither of them said a word, but Emily felt a sudden surge of love and confidence flow between them.

And for the first time in months, Emily felt something rekindling inside her—the tiniest little spark of hope.

She was ready to face them now. However difficult it would be to face them, Emily was ready.

Thirteen

When Elizabeth walked into the living room, she couldn't believe how distraught Karen Mayer looked. "Where is she?" Karen cried, still holding Karrie tightly in her arms. "Where's Emily?"

"I'm right here," a clear voice said from the doorway. Emily was standing alone at the foot of the stairs, looking in at the assembly that had gathered: her father, Karen, Jessica, Elizabeth, Grandpa Wakefield, and Mr. and Mrs. Wakefield. Grandma Wakefield was standing behind her on the landing, listening.

Mr. Wakefield cleared his throat. "Why don't we all clear out of here and give the Mayers a chance to talk by themselves," he suggested, getting to his feet.

"No!" Karen cried, her voice almost hysterical. "I'm sorry," she said instantly, fighting for control. "But what I have to say needs to be said in front of everyone in this room. I owe

Emily an apology," she added, "and because of the way I've embarrassed her in front of her friends, I'd like the chance to apologize in front of you, too."

Emily reached out to grab hold of the wood framing the doorway. She felt unsteady all of a sudden. Karen . . . apologizing?

"If it weren't for Emily," Karen said brokenly, tightening her arms around little Karrie, "Karrie would be—" Tears ran down her cheeks. "Little Karrie would be dead right now if it weren't for Emily. She choked on a bead that fell off a toy I gave her, a toy that wasn't safe. And Emily noticed it wasn't safe! She warned me! But I was too pigheaded to notice. And even when I saw what happened, I didn't know how to save my own child. If it weren't for Emily . . ."

Karen broke down, her shoulders shaking as she wept. No one said anything, and Emily felt dizzy. She couldn't believe what was happening.

"But that's only part of the story," Karen went on, lifting her tear-streaked face and moving her gaze around the circle of attentive faces. "Ever since I married Ron, I've been jealous of Emily. Ron adored her, and I couldn't stand how much attention he gave her. So I tried. . ."

"Why don't you sit down, Karen?" Mrs. Wakefield suggested gently, offering her a chair.

Karen shook her head. "No, thank you," she whispered. Clearing her throat, she continued. "I've never given Emily even a ghost of a chance," she murmured. "I wouldn't listen to her. I was unreasonable about her curfew, unreasonable about her drums. I made her feel"—she took a deep, quavering breath—"unwanted and unloved. And that's something that is just unforgivable. I don't know how I could have done it," she sobbed. "I was so selfish! All I could think about was how much easier it would be for me if Emily was out of the house. So I started to threaten her with sending her to boarding school.

"I was the one who was threatened, though," she added tearfully, looking imploringly at the sympathetic faces around her. "I felt threatened because Emily was so capable. She knew everything about running the house, and I didn't know a thing! Even with Karrie—she seemed to be so good around the baby. And I felt insecure.

"Emily," Karen said brokenly, "I'm so sorry. Can you forgive me?"

The next thing Emily knew, she was crying, too. But she wasn't standing in the doorway anymore. She had both her arms around Karen and little Karrie.

"Daddy," Emily managed, turning finally to her father.

Mr. Mayer crossed the room in two giant steps, engulfing his wife and both his daughters in an enormous hug. For the first time since she was a little girl, Emily felt that she was part of a family, a real family, with a father *and* a mother.

It was like stepping inside the photograph she had always treasured. Only this time, she told herself fiercely, they were all going to stay together. They were going to make it work, the way Grandma Wakefield and Louis had. And nothing would ever separate them, not as long as they lived!

"This is going to be the best surprise dinner ever." Jessica grinned as she used a long-handled spoon to taste the gravy that was bubbling on the stove. "Mom, you were absolutely right about having a buffet. We'd never fit all these people in the dining room!"

"Well, we didn't know all the Mayers were coming." Mrs. Wakefield laughed. It was Saturday evening, and the twins were in the kitchen with their mother, putting the finishing touches on the food before carrying it out to their guests.

"I just hope the surprise I've planned for Emily goes all right," Elizabeth whispered to Jessica. "What if she's angry with me for interfering?"

"It would serve you right." Jessica giggled. "What time are the mysterious dinner guests supposed to arrive?" she demanded.

"I'm not sure," Elizabeth said, checking her watch. "Dan said it might take them a little while to get together and come over here."

"Liz," Emily said shyly, as she walked into the kitchen, "is there anything I can help you with? I feel so useless just sitting out in the living room!"

Elizabeth gave Jessica a warning look. "Not a thing," she told Emily cheerfully, making a shooing motion to send her away. Emily looked like a different person, she thought, smiling. She looked happy and relaxed.

"I'd like to propose a toast," Mr. Wakefield said when the entire group was assembled in the living room. He cleared his throat, looking around at the expectant faces. "To families," he said finally, catching his parents' gazes and smiling at them.

"To families," Mr. Mayer echoed loudly, putting his arm around Emily.

"To mothers and daughters!" Karen called out, her eyes shining.

"I second that one!" Mrs. Wakefield beamed at the twins.

"Not to mention grandparents," Elizabeth added. "I'm going to miss you two so much!"

"You can always hot-air balloon over to Michigan." Grandma Wakefield chuckled.

Elizabeth groaned. "No, thanks."

Just then the door bell rang. "I'll get it," Elizabeth said hastily, hurrying out of the living room to open the front door.

"Come on in," she said under her breath. "Have you got them?" she asked Dan, taking his coat. "Hi, everybody!" she said to the

147

others—Guy Chesney, Max Dellon, and Dana Larson. "I'm so glad you all could make it!"

"Are you kidding?" Max grinned. "We're desperate to get Emily back. Do you know how horrible we sound without our drummer?"

"We've got them right here," Dan said. He and Guy went outside, and they returned a few moments later, carrying the drum cases. "Where should I put them?"

Elizabeth thought fast. "Let's set them up in the dining room," she whispered. "Come on, guys—but we've got to be quiet!"

Ten minutes later the Wakefields' dining room had been transformed. Elizabeth stood back to survey their work. Emily's drums were set up in the corner. All of the electric outlets were taken up by amplifiers, speakers, and the cords to Max's and Dan's guitars. But at last everything was ready.

"Dinner is served!" Elizabeth called, standing at the doorway to the living room and waving grandly in the direction of the dining room. "Emily, why don't you go in first?" she suggested, barely able to suppress a smile.

Emily looked at her strangely, but she obediently walked into the dining room. The next minute, Dana threw on the lights, and The Droids burst into one of their most popular songs. Max was on the guitar, Guy Chesney on the keyboards, and Dan, his eyes fixed on Emily, was on the bass guitar.

"My drums!" Emily cried, the color draining from her face. She stared at Dan. "But I thought. . ."

Dan shrugged, smiling. "Jamie changed his mind," he told her. "Do you think you can change yours?"

"Dan Scott!" Emily yelled, racing across the room and throwing her arms around his neck, "you are the most wonderful guy in the whole world!"

And the next thing anyone knew, Emily was behind her drums—where she'd always been happiest. And The Droids were playing while everyone, Karen and Mr. Mayer included, clapped to the beat.

Emily Mayer couldn't believe it. She skipped her drumsticks lightly across the taut surface of the drums. She could feel everything in her lighten as the music took over. Across the room, Karen and her father were smiling at her.

And Dan was beside her, playing better than she'd ever heard him before.

"We'd make a pretty good duet, you and me," he whispered when the song was over.

Emily didn't answer. Her heart was too full. But the look she gave him said it all. She had a feeling that the two of them were going to make some pretty special music together.

It had been a long, long time since Emily Mayer had been this happy. But she had a feeling that this was only the beginning!

*   *   *

Elizabeth was driving to the mall on Sunday afternoon, enjoying the beautiful day. She was supposed to meet Jessica at Lisette's, and she was really looking forward to it. It would be fun to relax.

Driving slowly through the beautiful neighborhood, Elizabeth ran over the events of the past week. She felt filled with contentment. She was so happy that Emily was finally reunited with Karen and her family.

A car honked at her, and Eddie Strong waved from his light brown Ford as he turned the corner. Elizabeth waved back, her aqua eyes thoughtful. Seeing Eddie reminded her that she still hadn't stopped by to see Regina.

Maybe I can visit her now, she said to herself, glancing at her watch. She'd told Jessica she'd meet her at three-thirty. She still had plenty of time. Turning the red Spider into the nearest driveway and checking her rear-view mirror, she began to back up and turn around.

The mall can wait, Elizabeth thought. She just wanted to run over to the Morrows'. It seemed it would be rude not to say hello to Regina and welcome her back to Sweet Valley.

Five minutes later she had reached the turn in the road where the Morrows' driveway began. Ordinarily the drive was open, but that day wrought-iron gates were closed—and padlocked. There was no sign of life.

150

"That's strange," Elizabeth said aloud. "I wonder if . . ." Her voice trailed off uncertainly. Could Eddie have been wrong about Regina? It sure didn't look as if anyone were home.

On an impulse Elizabeth decided to take a quick detour to Bruce Patman's house, which was only a few minutes away. If Regina really *was* back, Bruce would surely know all about it.

Twenty minutes later Elizabeth was out on the patio overlooking the Patmans' gorgeous, Olympic-sized swimming pool. Bruce had been swimming laps, and he wrapped himself in a towel to join her on the deck's surface.

To Elizabeth's surprise, Bruce hadn't heard a word about Regina's visit to Sweet Valley. "That's impossible!" he said when Elizabeth told him what Eddie had reported. "She's in the middle of a new set of treatments. There's no way she could leave Bern right now."

Elizabeth was completely baffled. "But Eddie seemed so sure," she told him. "He said she was back in town with her aunt. Do you think—"

"Wait a minute," Bruce interrupted. He padded across the patio and disappeared into the house. A minute later he was back, a cordless phone in his hand.

"My father's latest toy," Bruce explained and smiled, showing her the phone. "Designed for people too lazy to budge. You can keep the phone next to you wherever you go."

"Don't let my sister find out about that," Elizabeth said. "That's all we need!"

Bruce sat down in a lounge chair and tapped seven numbers out on the receiver. "You said Eddie claimed she was here with her aunt?" he asked Elizabeth while the phone rang.

Elizabeth nodded.

"Oh, hello," Bruce said into the phone. "This is Bruce calling—Bruce Patman. I just heard from a friend that Regina is in town, and I was kind of surprised. Can you tell me where she is?"

"She isn't here," a curt, unfamiliar voice told him. "I'm sorry."

Bruce's brow furrowed. "Who am I speaking with, please?" he asked politely.

"This is Regina's aunt," the woman told him. The next thing Bruce heard was a click as the receiver was put down—and a dial tone.

"That's odd," he said a moment later, his brow still wrinkled as he stared off across the emerald green of the Patmans' lawn.

"What's odd?" Elizabeth demanded, leaning forward.

"Whoever answered the phone said she was Regina's aunt," Bruce said, concern in his voice. "But Regina doesn't have an aunt. Both her mother and father are only children."

Elizabeth's heart skipped a beat. "Bruce, do you think something funny is going on?" she asked, the image of the locked gates at the Morrow estate flashing into her mind.

Bruce got to his feet. "I don't know," he said, his voice serious. "But I'll tell you this much—I intend to find out!"

What has happened to Regina Morrow, and who is her mysterious "aunt"? Find out in Sweet Valley High #26, HOSTAGE!

WINNERS

THIS EXCITING NEW SERIES IS ALL ABOUT THE THREE MOST ENVIED, IMITATED AND ADMIRED GIRLS IN MIDVALE HIGH SCHOOL: STACY HARCOURT, GINA DAMONE AND TESS BELDING. THEY ARE WINNERS—GOLDEN GIRLS AND VARSITY CHEERLEADERS—YET NOT EVEN THEY CAN AVOID PROBLEMS WITH BOYFRIENDS, PARENTS, AND LIFE.

☐ **THE GIRL MOST LIKELY (WINNERS #1) 25323/$2.25**

Stacy Harcourt is the captain of the varsity cheerleading squad, but she wants to break from her rigid, boring image as "Miss Perfect." But in doing so will she lose the friendship of Gina and Tess and the captainship of the squad? Or will she realize that maybe her "perfect" life wasn't so bad after all. 25323/$2.50

THE ALL AMERICAN GIRL (WINNERS #2)

Gina Damone has problems keeping up socially with the other cheerleaders because of her immigrant parents old-world attitudes. But when she begins dating All-American Dex Grantham his breezy disregard for her parents' rules makes her question his sincerity.—*Coming in February 1986.*

THE GOOD LUCK GIRL (WINNERS #3)

Cute, cuddly Tess Belding is the first student from Midvale's vocational-technical program ever to make the cheering squad, but she's going to be benched unless she can pass her French midterm! *Coming in May 1986.*